# MoveMind

by

Robert New

Tale Publishing

*Sever-Reign* first published by the City of Monash as 'Highly Commended' from the 2017 Wordfest Short Story Competition.     http://tinyurl.com/ycsnn4dx

*The Patriotic Amnesiac* first published in View from the Hill (Anthology), Tale Publishing, 2016.

*First Constant* is a chapter from *The Conversationist* rewritten as a short story.



First Published 2018
Copyright © 2018 Robert New
All rights reserved.

National Library of Australia Cataloguing-in-Publication entry:
Creator: New, Robert, author.
Title: MoveMind / Robert New.
ISBN: 978-0-6480386-7-2 (paperback)
Subjects: Speculative fiction short stories.

Tale Publishing
Melbourne Victoria

## Other Books by Robert New

Incite Insight
The Conversationist
View from the Hill (Contributor)


## Dedication

For my family. For Caroline, not because I said I would, but because I want to. For the friends and people who keep asking when they can read the next story.

# Contents

# How to Win a War

'You will be tortured,' Abdul Abassi said to his captive. 'And this torture will produce within you a great conflict. You will question what you value and what you believe in and you will want it to end. At this point we will ask you to do something for us and you will agree, because at that point you will want to do what we ask.'

Captain Simon Briggs shuddered involuntarily and wondered if he'd died and gone to hell. Standing face-to-face with his captor he was close enough to smell the Koresh stew on Abdul's breath. He knew with certainty that he hated him.

'The torture will begin in three months' time on April

7<sup>th</sup>, once you've had a chance to heal.'

Briggs involuntarily clutched his left leg. It had been badly broken and lacerated when his helicopter was hit by a rocket. The milk run he'd been promised had turned into something else entirely.

'After all, we want you to be strong enough to withstand it…'

Abdul smiled. 'So, we know who you are from your dog tags, but what we don't know is if you have any family. Do you?'

Adbul leaned in closely for Briggs' response. Briggs shuddered again and pictured his wife, Anna, and their infant daughter, Lizzie. He tried to imagine never seeing them again.

'No,' he said firmly. There was no way he was going to let his captors use them against him. Apparently satisfied with the answer, Adbul spun on his heels and left the room.

Briggs hobbled to his bed and sat down, carefully lifting his leg onto the mattress. Every time he looked at his leg he recalled the crash. The rocket had seemed to come from nowhere and had probably been fired by a shoulder mounted RPG. It had destroyed the chopper's tail rotor and bent the main blades, causing the craft to spiral to the ground. Each spin had accentuated the fear Briggs felt and he'd thought with certainty that he was going to die. The fall took seventeen seconds, but when the impact came it wasn't as catastrophic as he'd expected. The partially functioning primary rotor had slowed the fall. When the helicopter hit the ground, left side down, his co-pilot had been killed and Briggs had wound up on top of him. Enemy soldiers had pulled him, barely conscious, from the wreck.

Briggs looked at his leg. They'd done a good job with it, but Briggs guessed he would always have a limp. The bandages were wrapped so tightly they were almost like a cast, yet could be changed regularly to allow the lacerations to heal.

He thought about what Abdul had said and wondered why they were waiting for his leg to heal before they tortured him. Any information he had would be out of date by then. What could they possibly hope to get from him? He'd rather die than tell them anything.

Briggs looked around the room, which was surprisingly modern and comfortable. The walls were white, and there was a bookcase with an assortment of English language books. The bedding was clean and pressed and the mattress comfortable. In an open corner of the room there was a toilet and shower. The only clues he was a captive were the bars on the windows, the metal door and the lack of privacy around the shower and toilet. He remembered a time he and Anna had holidayed in Guam. The room they'd paid for was worse than this.

Anna. God, he hoped she was okay. What must she be thinking? She probably thought he was dead. He would get back to her. He thought this as hard as he could, willing the thought and the message that he was alive to travel across the world and reach her. Then he lay down and cried for the first time since his daughter was born. He must have fallen into an exhausted sleep, for when he awoke there was a steaming bowl of a thick soup and a white drink waiting for him. With them was a folded card that stated: In Farsi, this dish is called āsh-e anār. It is a soup. The drink is called doogh. Briggs felt a wave of hunger. How long had it been since the crash? It would seem unnecessary to drug or poison him, so why not try the food?

He cautiously tasted the soup. Its flavour and consistency were not what he was used to, but it was pleasant and felt nourishing. The pomegranate seeds in it added a sweetness and crunch that was appealing. A while after he'd finished the soup, he tried the milky coloured drink. Its taste was odd, almost toothpaste like; it was as though someone had crushed some mint and blended it with yoghurt and soda water. Briggs hadn't tasted anything quite like it before.

#

The next day Briggs was mostly left alone. Abdul stood by the door as guards changed his bandages and dropped off food. They smiled at Briggs, but it was clear that

Abdul was the only one who spoke English. Briggs was grateful when they changed his bandage as it was beginning to smell. When they unwrapped his leg, even though he knew it was badly damaged, the sight of the wounds made his mind reel. Scabs had formed over the cuts but many were weeping pus and the bruising and swelling made it seem as though the leg were not his own. The guards handed him some pills and some doogh to drink.

'They're painkillers and antibiotics to control the infection,' Abdul said from the doorway. 'They will help you feel better and get well.'

'So you can torture me?'

'So you can be tortured,' Abdul confirmed with a smile.

'Why wait? Why not do it now?' He held his breath, not sure he wanted to know the answer.

'Captain Briggs, we are not trying to win the battle, we are trying to win the war.' Briggs noticed Abdul's British accent for the first time and surmised that he'd probably been educated in London.

'What does that mean?'

'You will see in just under three months. In the meantime you have stable fractures of your tibia and fibula, so stay off your leg. The mattress is memory foam and should help relieve some of the pressure on it.'

Briggs marvelled at how Abdul managed to make it

sound as though he cared. He barked an order at the guards in a language Briggs didn't understand. They nodded and moved the bookcase next to the bed, and then all of them left the room.

Briggs looked at the titles. It was an odd assortment of books, all were dog eared and worn. There were books on philosophy, biology, and the history of science. There was also poetry, two Sherlock Holmes collections and an English translation of the Qur'an. The oddest book was an encyclopaedia of bodybuilding, written by a former Mr. Olympia. The book was heavy enough to be used as a weight. Briggs picked up a Sherlock Holmes book and began to read. Maybe it was the drugs kicking in, but hell was beginning to look not so bad.

#

Briggs spent the next three days reading the Sherlock Holmes books. A few minutes after he'd finished the last story, the metal door creaked open and Abdul strode into the room, flanked by two guards.

'Captain, you have not been open with me.'

'What do you mean?'

'My guards tell me that you moan when you go to toilet.'

'My leg hurts when I walk over there,' Briggs said. Abdul moved closer to Briggs and looked him in the eye. In a warm, fatherly voice he asked 'Yes, but it's more than that isn't it?'

The tone of Abdul's voice drew him in and any notion of lying disappeared, 'I have diarrhoea,' Briggs admitted sheepishly. 'The cramps and gas movement are painful and aggravate the pain in my leg.'

If I told him that just because he asked nicely, then what will I tell him when he tortures me? Briggs thought glumly.

'Hmph,' Adbul turned to the guards and barked an order in what he now knew was Farsi. One of them immediately left the room.

'We cannot move your bed or the toilet, as they are fixed in place, so you will have to put up with hobbling over. The guard will bring you some crutches. It was an oversight not to provide them earlier. Oh, and someone else will visit you shortly. It will not be pleasant, but we need to … gauge … what you can withstand, so that your effectiveness in twelve weeks' time is improved.'

Briggs felt a ripple of apprehension. Abdul gestured in the direction of a book by the bed. 'Finished?'

'Yes.'

'Try the book on philosophy next. I enjoyed it,' Abdul said matter-of-factly.

'Okay. So are these your books?'

'Yes. I accumulated them when I studied in England. It was a simpler time back then,' he said, as though he genuinely missed it. 'I wish more of my countrymen could spend time there. Anyway, I have another prisoner to check on. His torture begins in a few hours. I almost feel sorry for him. It will be tough. I'll see you tomorrow.' Abdul strode from the room.

Briggs shuddered. How could a person be so blasé about torture? How could he go from seeming so human to so inhumane?

Briggs lay down and tried to sleep, but his mind kept drifting between his family and the fate that awaited him. He wept. God, he missed Anna and Lizzie. What if he never saw Lizzie again? Or heard her speak or watched her learn to walk? What torture could be worse than that?

Just as he was on the verge of sleep, a guard and a second man came into the room. The second man identified himself as a doctor and proceeded to check Briggs' leg.

'It seems to be on the path to healing. Do try and keep weight off it though. The fractures are well aligned, but they went right through the bones, so they could easily go out of alignment.' The doctor's speech had an accent that Briggs couldn't place. At least his tone was friendly.

'This next bit will hurt,' the doctor said as though he would enjoy what happened next. He held up an odd metallic device. It was almost like a comb, except the prongs were spaced apart. Each prong had its own liquid filled cap on the end. The doctor slowly removed each cap one-by-one, heightening Briggs' apprehension. The guard grabbed Briggs' arm and forcefully pulled up the sleeve of his T-shirt. In one swift movement the doctor scraped the device across Briggs' upper arm. Each prong caused a shallow cut, and blood oozed from each wound. The pain caused Briggs to gasp.

The next day the doctor returned with Abdul and repeated the procedure on Briggs' other arm. Abdul watched closely, never taking his eyes off Briggs' face. It was as though he wanted to see Briggs' response to the pain. Briggs was determined not to let his fear show, and this time he did not cry out. The doctor and Abdul exchanged some words in Farsi. It seemed as though Abdul was not happy with what he had seen.

That night the doogh tasted subtly different. Briggs couldn't quite identify why. If they are poisoning him, should he care? He thought of Anna and Lizzie, decided he should, and convinced himself it was just a different type of mint.

#

During the next two weeks Abdul visited Briggs every day and, although their exchanges were short, it seemed to Briggs that Abdul was trying to make him as comfortable as possible. There had been no more instances of the doctor or his comb.

Abdul and the guards handled the care of his leg, and

the lacerations gradually stopped weeping. Briggs tried hard to remind himself he was a prisoner. He spent his time composing messages in his head to his wife and daughter, and reading the books Abdul had provided. Several of them had been quite enlightening, but the threat of the forthcoming torture meant Briggs never quite relaxed. By the fourth week, he had mastered using his crutches and was quite mobile within his room. He no longer needed to use the toilet with such urgency, which meant he could get there without aggravating his injury.

Six weeks after the crash things began to change. Abdul arrived one morning with four guards and a wheelchair.

'Captain, I imagine you are going a bit … stir crazy … being trapped in here all day.'

Briggs nodded, dumbfounded.

'So I propose that we go out.'

Briggs wondered if he was being set up and was about to be led someplace he didn't want to go, but Adbul seemed so sincere. He felt his face betray his confusion. 'Why are you being nice to me?'

'Captain Briggs, in six weeks you will suffer greatly. As I said before, you will question what you value and what you believe. What will make it easier for us to produce this conflict within you, is if you feel a friendship towards us. The torture will make you want to return to this state of friendship. How else can we get you to want to do what we ask? Plus, charity is a means of self-purification and Allah knows I need that.'

Briggs realised the honesty of the statement and tried not to cringe. It was true they had provided for his basic needs of food, health and shelter, but now he realised they were also helping him feel cared for and connected. I will never help you, Briggs thought, although he felt his conviction waning.

'There is also something else you need to know. When you crashed just over the border from Afghanistan, you were semi-conscious for quite some time. You are no longer near the border or your base, in fact you are quite far north. You are in a city called Babolsar and just a kilometre from the Caspian Sea. So how about we go and have a look around?'

Briggs nodded, unable to speak.

The guards helped him into the wheelchair and one wheeled him while two others flanked him. The fourth guard stayed close to Abdul which made Briggs think he must be important. They wheeled him around the city, and every time they turned a corner Briggs was startled. The place was surprisingly modern. It was still dated, but nothing like the mud brick, ramshackle city Briggs had pictured. The biggest shock was how lush and green it was, especially compared to the desert Briggs had been flying over when he'd been shot down. He wished he'd never crossed the border even though he'd been ordered to do so.

The people he passed smiled at him and seemed pleased to see him, which surprised Briggs too, as, despite the length his beard had grown, he was still clearly a foreigner. Weren't these people meant to be his enemy?

The group approached an arched bridge which looked like a much smaller version of the Sydney Harbour Bridge. They turned right and followed the river to the sea. Briggs saw several people fishing from narrow boats. Abdul was mostly silent during the journey, letting the city speak for itself. As they returned to the prison Briggs was left with the distinct impression that Babolsar was a thriving coastal town.

#

Over the next five weeks, Briggs was taken out every day. He was encouraged to interact with the local people and learnt how to say enough phrases in Farsi to order lunch and say thank you. The guards played board games with him in the evening, which worked despite the language barrier. Abdul would discuss the books Briggs had been reading, which made Briggs realise he'd started to enjoy reading them. The more he read and learnt about the range of subjects, the more he felt he was gaining an appreciation of aspects of humanity that his education had lacked. This boosted his self-esteem and made him wonder if perhaps Abdul was revealing too much of himself by providing and discussing the ideas. After all, if he understood how Abdul saw the world, then surely he'd be able to use that to his advantage when the torture started. The forthcoming torture was never far from his mind and he often wondered what form it would take. Would they cut him like they had before? Use electrodes? Waterboarding? He hoped there wouldn't be waterboarding. Drowning had been one of his biggest fears since childhood when he'd been jokingly held under water by a friend who hadn't realised he'd run out of air. Briggs shivered at the thought.

#

By April 6th, his leg had healed well enough to walk short distances without crutches. Briggs was lying on his bed reading the Qur'an, the last book from the shelf. Abdul entered and sat on the end of the bed. He carried a fresh pile of clothes.

'So what are you finding out by reading that?' he asked softly.

'I don't know. I guess that your religion is actually one of peace.'

'It is,' Abdul confirmed.

'So that confuses me.'

'How so?'

'Aren't you going to torture me tomorrow?'

Abdul grinned slyly. 'Me?'

'Yes.'

'I never said I, or even we, would be the ones to torture you.'

'But what about the scratching of my arms?' Briggs asked doubtfully.

Abdul laughed. 'Yes, it was probably wrong of me not to explain what was going on there, but revealing our plan for you too early would have undermined the effect of you piecing it together for yourself.'

'What was it about then?'

'You had diarrhoea.'

'Yes, I did.'

'Well that was illogical. You were on strong painkillers which should have had the opposite effect. Let me suggest something to you— diarrhoea was not uncommon for you.'

Briggs was shocked by the accurate assumption and only then realised how healthy he was feeling in both body and mind. It was the healthiest he'd felt in years.

'We are aware that such a disturbance is often indicative of an allergy or food intolerance, so we tested you. The scratchings were standard tests for common allergies, and in fact it is much nicer to have them done in one hit rather than individually. I allowed you to think of it as a prelude to torture to maintain your expectation that we were bad people.'

'But why?'

'So that your understanding of us, our culture and way of life would develop … organically … and despite your preconceived notions of who we were. The conflict between what you believed before you met us, and what you experienced in the city must have caused you some angst?'

'It did.'

'And how do you feel about us now?'

Briggs stopped to think about what he'd been asked. The range of emotion was surprising. Eventually, Briggs simply said, 'I like you.' It was as much an admission of his journey from enemy to friend as it was a summation of his feelings.

'Excellent. Have a shower and trim your beard. You will be leaving our care now … so I'm afraid this is goodbye.'

'Huh?'

'A car will take you Tehran, where you are booked on a flight to Abu Dhabi in the United Arab Emirates. We have contacted your embassy there. They will meet you when you get off the plane. Unfortunately, this flight is necessary as America no longer has an embassy in my country. You are going home. When you are in the car open this.' Abdul handed him an envelope and smiled. When he stood to leave, Briggs followed. Abdul spread his arms for a hug and, with an eagerness that surprised him, Briggs responded. The embrace set off a wave of emotions. To his further surprise, Briggs felt tears welling in his eyes.

'So long, my friend,' Abdul said softly.

As Abdul left the room, Briggs' heart surged. My God. He was going home to Anna and Lizzie. He felt a fresh wave of emotion and openly cried. What if they were only giving him hope as a way to break him? Somehow, Briggs couldn't see Abdul lying about this, despite it making sense as a way of starting the torture. Five minutes later he had composed himself enough to follow the instruction to shower and trim his beard. As the water flowed over him, he felt cleansed and freer than ever before. He dried off and dressed in the fresh clothes Abdul had provided. When he was ready, he opened his door. The guards escorted him to a waiting car. The car, an IKCO Samand, was new and clean. Inside was a cane made from cypress, with a card attached. It read:

*This cane is a gift to you. You will be taking route 77 to Tehran. It is not the most direct route, but will give you a more scenic journey and time to contemplate.*

The car set off. Briggs wondered if he'd ever hear from Abdul again. Briggs suddenly remembered he still had one last message from Abdul: the envelope. He reached into his pocket and pulled it out. Inside was a single piece of thick beige paper upon which was a handwritten message. Briggs admired the penmanship.

*Dear Captain,*

*The circumstances which brought you to us were unfortunate. However, I hope that your stay with us was not too painful, even though I know the separation from your country and loved ones would have been hard on you. Please understand that we are trying to end the war and that in order to do so we needed to detain you for a while.*

*I mentioned to you that we would have a request of you and it is this: share your thoughts of us with others in your country and help others understand our religion and way of life if they speak out of ignorance.*

*I hope you understand why we did what we did and forgive us for holding you.*

*I hope your leg recovers fully.*

*Warmest regards.*

*Your Friend,*

*Abdul Abassi*

*By the way you are lactose intolerant. We added lactase to any dairy products you were given. You may want to continue doing that when you are back in America.*

Throughout the four hour drive from Babolsar to Tehran, Briggs experienced the full range of emotions. When he had first been captured, being set free was all he could think about. Now he was almost sad to leave. The books, conversation and kindness shown to him had made Briggs feel like a better human being.

#

When they arrived at the airport, Briggs felt another surge of excitement. He wondered if this was really happening, or just a sick prelude to torture. Maybe he'd just lost it? The guard parked in a restricted space at the front of the airport and escorted Briggs inside. He presented official papers to the airport security personnel and they waved the two of them through. The guard explained in accented English that he would stay with Briggs until he was on the plane to make sure customs would let him fly and not arrest him.

As Briggs handed over his boarding pass, the flight attendant commented, 'That is a magnificent cane.'

'Yes, it is.' Briggs replied, taking the time to admire its craftsmanship.

'Wood is a scarce commodity in this country you know,' the attendant said. 'So how bad is your leg?'

'It's much better now, but it was badly broken a while ago.'

'How long?'

'Three months.'

'And you have just been cleared to fly,' the attendant said matter-of-factly. Briggs felt the confusion show on his face.

'Well, usually you have to wait three months to fly otherwise you risk developing clots, plus the usual swelling you get from flying can interfere with the healing process.' The attendant said this as though it was a statement learnt by rote.

Briggs felt as though the floor was turning to liquid under his feet. Three months. He'd not been allowed to fly for three months! His mind reeled at the thought. They'd kept him only until he was well and healthy enough to fly home.

Briggs spent the flight thinking about and re-evaluating his stay in Iran. He now thought of it more as a visit rather than an imprisonment.

The flight was smooth and uneventful. When he disembarked from the plane, two American men approached.

'Captain Simon Briggs?' one queried.

'Yes.'

'I'm Tom Smith and this is James Anderson. We're from the US Embassy. We understand you were held captive and have just been released.'

'Yes.'

'Were you treated well?'

'Yes.'

'And they just let you go?' Smith asked as though he already knew the answer.

'Yes.'

'What did they ask you?'

Briggs stopped. At no point had they asked him anything about the army or for any information related to the war.

'Nothing,' Briggs replied, expecting to be disbelieved.

'They keep doing this,' Anderson muttered loud enough for Briggs to hear.

'There were others? How many others have been held like me?'

'You make two thirteen.'

'Wow.' Briggs tried to grapple with the potential consequences. Imagine if there were thousands or tens of thousands. The relationship between America and Iran would change completely. It really could end the war.

'Would you like to call your wife?' Anderson asked, handing him a phone.

With a trembling hand Briggs dialled. Anna answered on the third ring.

'Hello?'

'Hello, Anna.' He felt a wave of relief and happiness surge through him. It was so good to hear her voice.

'Oh, Simon, it's so great to hear you after all this time.'

Briggs was surprised. She sounded happy but not as overcome as he'd expected.

'You don't seem surprised that I'm alive.'

'I thought you'd died when we were told your helicopter had been shot down. It was horrible. I couldn't bring myself to tell Lizzie. I kept holding out hope that there was some kind of mistake, and then a miracle happened. A letter arrived from someone named Abdul Abassi. Do you know him?'

'Yes.' Briggs choked up. Abdul had let his family know he was alive so that they wouldn't suffer.

'He said you were injured and they would help you recover and return you to us on April 7th.' Briggs realised he'd arrive back in America on that date. But wasn't that the date his torture was meant to begin?

'He gave us an IP address, and when we typed it into the browser we could see you on a webcam.'

'You could see me?'

'Yes, for a few hours each day. The army guys couldn't trace it. I've never known you to read so much.'

'You knew I was okay?'

'Yes. The note also apologised for the delay in letting us know you were all right, but apparently you told them we didn't exist and without our names it was harder to track us down. Don't worry I understand why,' Anna said with a smile in her voice. 'The embassy has said you'll arrive at 6.00pm tomorrow. Lizzie and I will meet you at the airport. She's looking forward to seeing you. I think she's been wondering why she could see Daddy but not talk to him. She's rolling over now, I can't wait for you to see. I've missed you so much. I love you, Honey.'

Briggs handed the phone back to Anderson and cried. His family hadn't suffered while he'd been gone!

Thank you Abdul. Thank you. Thank you.

'We have a military plane waiting for you. You'll go home via Bagram Airfield in Afghanistan,' Smith said.

'You mean I'm not getting on a commercial flight? I just got off one.'

'Yessir,' Smith replied, monosyllabically.

#

The flight to Bagram was fast and uneventful. Briggs was greeted as a hero at the base. A Major greeted him and spoke quietly to him. 'Did you know we have some of them here?' The Major said them with such distaste that Briggs was shocked. 'Would you like to see them?' the major asked.

'Yes.' The Major guided Briggs to a secret underground jail, which had been added in 2009. Briggs was shocked. The cells were dirty and overcrowded, and the prisoners were using buckets for toilets. The prisoners watched the two of them with hatred in their eyes. Some were clearly just villagers. There were even women and children in the cells. All Briggs could think was that this wasn't how you should treat people. It took a lot for him to stop himself trying to set them free.

'Can you see how much they hate us? How much they fear us?' The Major sounded proud of the achievement. Briggs realised Abdul was right. This wasn't how you won a war.

'You know, making them hate us even more is not

how you end the war.'

'Huh?' The Major looked at Briggs as though he'd lost his mind.

'They didn't treat me like this.'

'So you're one of them now?'

Briggs hesitated and then indicated the prisoners. 'No, but they are not the enemy.' He realised the government did not represent the people, who just wanted to live their lives in peace.

The Major's voice rose. 'Are you saying we are?'

'No. Ignorance is the enemy,' Briggs said with the rush of an epiphany, 'Excuse me, I have to catch a flight. Can you take me back please?'

The Major grunted and took Briggs back to the airfield.

#

That night Briggs started the first leg of his flight to America. Try as he might, he couldn't sleep, and he barely noticed the day change over to April 7th. He thought about how he'd been greeted in the streets by the everyday people of Babolsar. No one had seemed angry with him, or fearful, despite his Western appearance. They had smiled and welcomed him. If hundreds of soldiers had been through the same thing as him, then the Babolsarians were learning as much about Americans as they had about them. Briggs could only think, with regret, how much his own people alienated minorities and made little effort to get to know them. Briggs felt nauseated. He was ashamed of his people. Fragments of conversations floated into his mind: "This torture will produce within you a great conflict. You will question what you value and what you believe in. We will ask you to do something for us and you will agree. You will want to do what we ask."

Briggs knew that Abdul had spoken the truth and that he would fulfil Abdul's request. There was certainly no way he could be part of a war against them. For Briggs, the war had ended.

# The Prophet of Social Media

Did gods create humans, or did humans create gods? Johnny didn't know and if it hadn't been for his brother-in-law the questions would never have come up. Despite seven years of religious education, Johnny was agnostic, but his teachers had at least managed to install a nagging doubt. Johnny had many thoughts about gods. A particular feature of gods was omnipresence. They saw everything we did. They knew our sins and our obedience. Johnny felt that for millennia, they had been figments of our imagination made real by the power of thought. He felt that this millennium a change had occurred. The new perception of gods was that they weakened us, deprived us of true freedom by setting dogmatic rules to follow. Increasingly, they were seen as arguments through which wars were started, horrendous acts were justified and social division was promoted. In short, gods were seen as a burden we could do without.

But humans need gods. They need them. They were created in the first place out of requirement. Our brains are hard wired for spirituality. Gods have helped us relate to each other, form more cohesive societies, and behave better, lest we incur their wrath, either in this life or the next. Johnny wondered what we were to do to sort it out? If we destroyed the gods we created, what would will fill their place? How would our needs be met? Johnny worried about such matters more than he should.

He reasoned that any such replacement must also have the same sense of omnipresence; they would have to know what we did. The replacement must have a mechanism for punishment if we transgressed and a means for judgement on how we led our lives. Rather than being an individual, this could be administered by a community who acted like gods and passed judgement on us, ideally in real time. This would necessitate constantly sharing our lives with those around us, but in this scenario who or what would be the new God? Would it be the community itself, or the social networking site which enabled people to achieve this?

Lately, Johnny thought LifeOpenBook.com had become a God. It had certainly had an impact upon his life like one. Ever since his brother-in-law, Darren, had tagged him in a picture on the site.

#

Darren, had taken him to see *Wonder Woman*. They'd enjoyed the movie and were discussing how refreshing it had been to see strong women not merely in a battle scene but as the main focus and winner of the fight. Two women overheard their conversation and joined in, leading to a pleasant banter about movies, the Bechdel test, and the role of women in society. Darren, being single, quickly asked them to get a coffee with him and his "absolutely brilliant" brother in law. Lisa and Fiona accepted, and they spent the next hour having a conversation which Johnny later realised was the most fun he'd had in ages.

After saying goodbye, Johnny and Darren walked to Darren's car. As they opened their doors, Darren suddenly blurted out, 'Dammit.'

'What?' Johnny noticed Darren's crestfallen face but couldn't think of anything they were missing.

'I didn't get Fiona's number.'

Johnny laughed. 'Why don't you put one of the selfie's we took on LifeOpenBook and see if anyone knows them?'

Darren immediately brightened up, 'Good idea as

always. I think I'll do that.'

'I prophesise that someone will.'

They both smiled.

#

Two days later Johnny was at work when he received a message from Darren saying a friend had recognized Fiona in one of the photos he'd posted asking for help identifying the women and that he, Fiona and Lisa were now all connected on LifeOpenBook. Johnny swiped away the message and opened the app to see friend requests from both women. He accepted them without hesitation, after all it would be rude not to, closed the app and went back to work. A short while later another message from Darren arrived to say he had a date with Fiona that night. He thanked Johnny for his advice to turn to the 'good book.' It ended with, 'I love LifeOpenBook!'

#

The next day Lisa sent Johnny a message saying that Darren had told Fiona that Johnny's marriage was in trouble and that if it did wind up breaking down, he should give her a call, or maybe just call anyway? When Johnny saw the message, he felt his face flush. He debated how to respond or whether to respond at all. His marriage was in trouble, and he was annoyed Darren had blabbed about it. However, he could use a sympathetic ear to talk to. What if that was what 'just call anyway' meant? Johnny went back to work without replying; telling himself he would do it later when he'd had more time to think about what to say.

#

That night Johnny threw his phone on the bed and jumped into the shower. The hot spray did a good job of washing away his focus on work and transitioning him to 'home' mode. He hoped Stacey and he could have a quiet evening together, without fighting for a change. That would be so nice. Johnny dried himself and put on a T-shirt and sweatpants, whilst wondering what he should say to Lisa on LifeOpenBook.

As he stepped out of the bathroom it became obvious that while Johnny was in the shower, Stacey had opened the LifeOpenBook app on his phone and seen the message from Lisa. She was sitting on the edge of the bed. She leapt up, glaring at him in a rage and thrust the phone in his face.

'What is the meaning of this?' she yelled.

'It's, um, a message.'

'Is this who you're leaving me for? How dare you tell my brother our marriage is in trouble? Why does she want you to call?'

'Umm … she's just someone Darren and I had a coffee with after the movie the other night. I haven't even responded to her.'

'Well are you going to? Why does she think our

marriage is in trouble?'

'Oh come on Stace, you know we've not been in a good place since Paris and it's only getting worse.'

'You bastard. Well, I'm not going to be the bad guy in all of this,' Stacey said. Johnny felt a thick, black wall of dread rise within him.

'What have you done?'

'I've copied that bitch's message and posted it on my timeline so the world can see you're the problem, not me.'

Johnny shook his head. 'Oh no.'

By airing their issues publicly Stacey had made resolving their differences more complicated.

Johnny grabbed his wallet and keys. 'I can't even look at you right now,' he said. 'I'll stay in a hotel tonight.'

He made sure he slammed the door on the way out and walked to his car imagining the shocked look on her face.

#

One thing about gods is that they don't always behave the way you'd expect. Sometimes the biases in our judgement of righteous action mean gods might judge us differently to how we'd expect. Sometimes, our shining paths are lit by flames. Johnny was amused to see the responses to Stacey's post the next morning. It was clear she'd expected to be perceived as a martyr and he was sure she'd be surprised by the vitriol posted on her page.

Her friends had commented that she should trust her husband and that she had no evidence he'd cheated. It was unfair of her to judge him for just receiving a message. They said she was the one jeopardizing their marriage by leaping to conclusions and displaying insecurity. One friend even outright called her stupid for focussing on the wrong part of the message – her husband had confided in his brother-in-law that their marriage was failing. They said she should get off her lazy ass and fix that, so the part Stacey was worried about wouldn't matter as it wouldn't go anywhere. The same friend also accused her of being the reason the marriage was failing. Johnny laughed when he read that. It served her right.

Johnny imagined how Stacey might react to receiving the message that she was a 'sinner' directly from no less an authority as the social network. He knew she'd be livid at first, but hoped that over a few hours she would come to the realisation that there was more than just a grain of truth to the comments on her page. He hoped that when faced with the glory of the network, she would have a Damascus moment, seek its countenance and amend her ways.

#

Historically, gods have been interventionist, but over the last few centuries, this notion has waned to the point where tales of such past actions are being seen as metaphor rather than literal intervention. This is where the social network holds the edge over traditional deities. Two hours later Johnny received the call he wanted from Stacey. The man made god had intervened.

# The Patriotic Amnesiac

Verity walked into a twelve storey building located on the edge of the city's central business district. Finding the way to her desk was a little more difficult than the day before when her new employer had shown her to it. Verity was startled to see a large envelope on her desk as she approached, making her think she had mistaken which desk was hers. The envelope was ordinary, a buff manila pouch, sealed with what looked like fingerprint free sticky tape. It was addressed to Verity Trouver at WestNews. Verity guessed the label was written using a ruler to form the letters. Verity looked at the envelope and frowned. Who would know she was there? The uncovering of a conspiracy and successful prosecution of the mastermind had given her a measure of fame and led to her being head hunted. They weren't going to announce she worked there until her first article was published. Not that she knew what or when that would be. Maybe someone was tracking her movements?

With some trepidation, Verity opened the envelope to reveal a single sheet of paper, upon which the word 'mist' was written in small, black type.

Verity smiled as her tension released.

'At least you're interesting,' she said to the paper. Verity wondered what it could mean. Was it a warning to her as in a 'mist' of poison? Was it someone playing a joke? Could it mean to spray it with water? Verity decided that was the most likely and began an unsuccessful search for a spray bottle. She figured putting the paper under a tap wouldn't be the right course of action. 'Mist' indicated that it needed to be more controlled.

'There's always another way,' she muttered to herself, echoing her mother's often-used phrase, as she determined a new plan of attack; one which would require her going up to the building's top floor balcony which she'd been shown the day before.

Verity was so preoccupied in her quest she barely noticed herself bump into a colleague near the lift. Verity heard him mumble, 'You may have been head hunted to work here, but you don't have to be rude.' She made a quick apology and kept going.

Verity was grateful the balcony was empty as she wouldn't have to explain why, in the middle of winter, she was about to switch on the fans that blew a mist of water to keep people cool in summer. The mist started quickly. Verity held the paper up to it and watched as words appeared on the page. She barely had time to read them before the paper began disintegrating.

*Within the secret branches of the government there is a person known as 'The Singularity.' The Singularity is a master of game theory and covert operations. People come to her safe in the knowledge their discussions will never be repeated or shared with anyone, even those from other agencies, regardless of the potential capture or interrogation of this person.*

*Their absolute certainty of the security of their conversations means they reveal all details, regardless of their degree of classification. She alone has complete clearance. The people who seek her advice receive unbiased and highly valuable strategic plans for covert operations.*

*The Singularity's impartiality and the security of what she reveals is based on two things:*

*1.    She has only a five-minute memory due to the surgical removal of part of her brain.*

*2.    She volunteered for the procedure.*

*Her real name is classified, but I met her last week and after meeting her and constructing an image of her face from memory, I found an image that identified her. I have reason to believe she is your mother and that you are looking for her. I hope you find her.*

   *-A Friend*

Verity's mind reeled. Her mum! Five years of fruitless searching and then from nowhere a clue. Why now? She wondered if her dad knew about this, as he also worked for the government. Although, Verity had grown up with the impression his and her mother's jobs were in different areas. Her father's devastation when her mum disappeared meant they'd hardly spoken since. Had someone shared this with her dad and he'd asked them to send the note to her?

Verity paced the balcony. The expansive view of the city didn't help her frustration. Her mum could be anywhere.

Verity frowned. Surgical procedures meant records. Records meant clues. The surgeon would probably be an army doctor, so she'd have no chance of finding them. She needed to find Henry Silcove. He was the only anaesthetist her mum would've trusted. But she hadn't spoken to him since her mum disappeared.

An internet search and two phone calls later and Verity was told Henry would call her back after he was out of surgery. Verity was driving home when her phone finally rang.

'Hello, this is Dr. Silcove. I'm returning your call.'

'*Salut*, Henry,' Verity said in an exaggerated French accent.

'Oh, so it's that Verity. Are you in the city?'

'Yes, King's P...'

'Meet me in one hour where our families used to dine.'

'Okay,' Verity barely managed to say before he ended the call.

#

An hour later, Verity was sitting at a table in a quiet section of *Parrhesia* restaurant sipping a coffee. She felt a rush of air as the door opened and looked up to see Henry. Her eyes widened in surprise at his appearance.

'*Salut*, Verity. I'm so sorry I didn't reach out to you when your mother disappeared. I couldn't bring myself to look into your eyes.' He seemed to notice her concerned expression. 'Yes, I know I'm a bit different. A lot greyer, balder and a bit thinner.'

'Henry, I can see ribs through your shirt. What the hell happened to you?' She momentarily forgot about her mother as concern for the person she used to affectionately call 'uncle' took over.

'Let's just say the last five years have not been kind; ever since...' He paused and looked at Verity, seemingly for confirmation. Verity nodded.

'Since you helped my mother that day. Yes, I received a note that said Mum had some kind of surgery. It implied that's why she disappeared. You're the only one she'd trust to anaesthetise her. She always said anyone with the right procedural knowledge could repair someone, but that controlling someone's pain, controlling their consciousness was an art. She thought you were a master.'

'I was … I guess I still am, but I'm not the same person. I mean, what they did to your mother that day. They took her from you, from everyone. They took her memory. I know she volunteered, but they still agreed to it.'

'That's what the note said. But what does it really mean? How do you take someone's memory?'

'The part of the brain that encodes information for storage in long term memory is called the hippocampus, and there's one in each half of the brain. They removed your mother's hippocampi, well, nearly all of each. As a result she only has the ability to hold new memories for a few minutes.'

Verity wondered if her mother would remember her, but the thought was too painful to ask.

'She can she remember the past?'

'I think most of it; she knew she'd likely lose between months and years of memories from before the surgery. She told me during the surgery that it was okay, she'd worked for eleven years prior to make sure she'd remember what was needed, whatever that was, in case she lost more memory than anticipated during the operation.'

That would explain why she'd always seemed so driven and somehow both present and absent. But why no contact from her? The idea that her mother didn't want to see her was hurtful, especially since her father had run off with their neighbour about the same time her mother disappeared. The only contact she'd had from him since was an annual birthday card.

'We knocked her out for the last part of the operation. When she woke up I asked her "what's the last thing you remember?"'

'And?'

'She was a bit groggy, but she said something about the view from the hill. She talked about the sun rising over the mountains and the mist in the valleys.'

Verity's hopes rose. It had been their special place. Maybe her mother had needed her.

'Mum used to take me there every Sunday morning. She always said she wanted to remember those moments forever.'

'Perhaps, now you know why?'

Verity frowned. 'I thought she was being cheesy. Do you know where she is?'

'No, I never saw or heard from her again and I was sworn to secrecy about what happened. I'm risking jail time talking to you about this, but I can't, I can't keep it to myself anymore.'

Verity could see how the secret had consumed him over the years.

'So you can't tell me anything else?'

'No. Only that she thought it would be easier for you and your father if she just disappeared.'

'Easier?' Verity felt an unexpected surge of anger. How could her mum think this would be easier?

Henry reached for her hand.

'Yes. But think about how heartbreaking it would be being around her now – when she couldn't remember what day of the week it was, what year it was, or anything about the last five years. Everything that you would tell her would be lost and your relationship would be permanently stuck in the past. She wouldn't be able to ask you how an important event went or show concern for dates or birthdays. People would notice the change in her and that would bring attention to her, which I'm guessing, given the non-disclosure forms I signed, would be a bad thing.'

Verity sighed. 'Yes, I guess so.'

'Perhaps you can answer one thing for me?' Henry asked.

'Of course.'

'Why did she do it? Why would she agree to have such a severe surgery?'

He asked with such intensity that Verity realised that

he felt he had to know the answer, despite the risk of repercussions from him asking.

'The note I received said that Mum works for the government, I kind of always had that impression. Dad too, but I never had any idea what branch. By removing her ability to form new memories, she became more useful to them.'

'And your mum was always so patriotic,' Henry added.

'Yes, country first, religion second, family third,' Verity said by rote. Both her parents had drilled it into her since childhood.

'Indeed.' Henry sighed. 'So what will you do now?'

'Figure out a way to find her, I guess.'

'For what it's worth, I don't think she told anyone else about the view. Maybe it was important to her for a reason?'

'That's possible. Given how much of a planner Mum was, if there's anything that's meant for me there, it would only reveal itself at what was our special place and time.' Memories of the lookout flooded over her, and tears welled in her eyes.

'Verity…' Henry said, his throat catching the word.

'Yes?'

'She'd told me the surgery was for a tumour. She only told me the real reason during the operation. I should have known something was up though, given the men in suits watching, but I didn't stop to think.'

'During?'

'Yes, she was conscious throughout.'

No wonder she'd insisted on him.

'It was the only way to know that they were operating in the right area. If I'd known what they were planning on doing … I'm so sorry. I would never…' The remorse was evident in his voice.

'I know' Verity reached reassuringly for his hand, then stood and gave him a hug.

'It's okay,' she said softly, 'It's not your fault.'

Henry sobbed as Verity gently kissed the top of his head.

'I have to go now,' she said, her voice suddenly hoarse. He nodded.

As soon as Verity was outside the restaurant, she broke down crying.

#

The next Sunday morning, Verity drove to the lookout at the top of a large hill near her childhood home. She arrived just before daybreak. The view was punctuated by streetlights, until the sun's orange rays shifted the palette of the scene. This was what she and her mother had found so enchanting; the kaleidoscopic change in what they could see over the hour or so of the sun rising from behind the mountains and the mist lifting in the valleys.

At the lookout point was a rock the size of a washing basket with the inscription: *The truth shall set you free.*

The rock was on the other side of a balustrade and on the edge of a steep drop.

Verity remembered the rock being put there a year or so before her mother disappeared. Her mother had never really said anything about it, other than regularly pointing out that it was a nice addition to the view.

Verity meant truth. Could this really be a message from her mother? She studied the inscription. The word 'the' seemed superfluous. Why include it unless it had another purpose? The more Verity thought about it the more it seemed as though the whole thing was meant for her, especially since her mother had mentioned it frequently.

Her mum was fond of hiding things in plain sight, so if it were a message it would be something obvious. Verity climbed on the balustrade, leant over and pressed each letter of the words 'the' and 'truth' in turn. Nothing happened. She frowned and tried again. Still nothing. Verity realised it would have to be something that wouldn't be triggered by a naughty child climbing on the rock. She spelt 'truth' on the letters of se<u>t</u>, f<u>r</u>ee, yo<u>u</u>, <u>th</u>e. This time the rock shifted back slightly from the edge of the cliff. Verity marvelled at how such a rock could be installed as she climbed onto it. Looking over the edge induced a strong sense of vertigo and Verity felt herself feel giddy. She started sweating as her nerves increased. The movement of the rock had revealed a slit in the ground, which contained what looked like a memory card sealed in clear plastic. Verity could almost reach it. She focussed on the card and tried not to think about what it would mean if she slipped. Finally, her fingers locked around the package and she shuffled back from the edge, breathing heavily. She stepped back over the balustrade and a minute later, the rock slid into its original place.

Verity decided to complete the old Sunday morning ritual she and her mother had shared. She drove to their favourite café and ordered Atlantic eggs and a cappuccino.

While she waited for her breakfast arrive, she took out her laptop and inserted the memory card. There was a single file present, but when Verity tried to open it, it asked for a password.

If the file was meant for her, what password would her mum have chosen?

She tried a few phrases and words without success.

As her mum liked to hide things in plain sight, perhaps the inscription on the rock was also a clue about the file. What was the phrase she used to use? Verily Verity?

Verity smiled as she realised this could also be the file's way of asking if it was her. She typed VerilyVerity,

and the file opened. Verity smiled. Her mum's puzzles
had always been easier to solve than her father's. The
thought of her father made her wonder if she was more
angry with him for abandoning her or her mother for
disappearing. Verity realised she could also attribute the
anger to whatever branch of the government they
worked for and prioritised above her.

*My Darling Verity,*

*I'm so sorry I had to disappear from your life. I know it
won't make any sense to you, but this is what was necessary
for our country to improve the function of its intelligence
organisations. By the time you get this I will be an amnesiac
and unable to form new memories. As I would not be able to
function independently and would stand out, I might be easily
identifiable to our country's enemies. This is why I'll be going
into a special protection program with the government. Rest
assured, I will be well cared for, as will you be when I pass. I
am assuming that if you read this, then your search for me
has gone beyond 'grieving daughter' to something greater. If
so, you can meet me at our special place on the Monday before
your birthday each year. You know what time. Understand
that I will not be the person you knew, nor will I know how
much time has passed. Please think carefully about whether
you want to meet me when I'm like this.*

*Love always,*

*Mum*

Verity shook her head in disbelief. How could her

mother possibly think that her daughter wouldn't want to see her? Why would she believe her country was more important than her family? Verity felt the rise of anger within her again. She knew meeting her mother might put them both at risk, but she wanted answers.

#

Verity had to wait two months for the Monday before her birthday. In that time, her mother was rarely out of her mind. She hardly slept the night before, and made her way to the lookout a full hour before sunrise. It was still dark as she sat on the bench overlooking the valley. As the first purple shimmer appeared on the horizon over the mountains, she became aware of several figures approaching. She watched an older women break away from two men in suits and walk vigorously towards her. Her gait gave her away.

'Mum!' Verity exclaimed.

'Hello, Verity. I'd forgotten how beautiful you are. I have missed you. I love you.' Her mother took her hand as she sat down.

'I have so many questions.' Verity looked at her mother intensely. Despite the mixed emotions she'd had over the years, now all she felt was her mother's love.

'I may not be able to answer them. In a few moments I won't remember we've spoken.'

'I still don't really get how that can be…'

'It's hard to explain, but more or less, the changes

that need to occur for long term memory storage never happen, as the part of my brain that tells the neurons to make new connections doesn't exist. I can only learn new procedures – you know, muscle memory, even though I don't remember learning the new information. I know this, not because they told me so, but because I expected it as an outcome of the surgery. But as you know, I've always believed there is another way to doing anything. Seeing you is producing a strong emotional response in me so there is a chance I'll remember…'

The bullet came from nowhere. It hit the back of her mother's head, travelled through her brain and out of her right eye socket. Blood spattered as far as the rock and its inscription. As her mother slumped forward, Verity screamed, 'Mum!'

#

When Verity returned to work two weeks later, she found another manila envelope on her desk. It was addressed the same way and contained another single sheet of paper. Verity took it straight to the misting fan and gasped as she read:

*Singularities lie at the heart of black holes. Nothing is meant to be able to escape a black hole's gravity. No information that goes in is meant to get out; it was the same with your mother; no information she was told was meant to be able to get back out due to the surgery she'd had. Unfortunately, a few months ago, she found another way, just* as physicists are still trying to do for black holes. She saw and kept a picture of you in the newspaper after your investigative success. There *must* have been just enough of her brain to enable the strength of the emotion produced to allow her to form a new memory. Thereafter, she was able to remember some things she was told by looking at your picture and adding the emotion generated to her short term memory. We only found out she was doing this when she created a solution for my agency that showed knowledge she shouldn't have had. Her security was no longer assured, but we couldn't tell her handlers without revealing information we didn't want them to have. She was a true patriot, who put her country's needs above her own. She knew the risks going in and that if she became able to form new memories she'd have to be eliminated. Unfortunately this task fell to me, because I was best placed to work out a way to get to her. She was well protected so we had to draw her into the open. I knew the only way would be through you. You were always her greatest strength and, therefore, also a weakness. I'm sorry for the loss and involving you in tracking her. Despite everything, I will miss her too.

Love,

Dad.

# The Doppelganger Gambit

It's said that somewhere in the world there is a person to whom we're so alike in appearance and manner they could be mistaken for us. Nashida Jones often wondered what her doppelganger was doing and if they, unlike her, were a mother. This New Year's Eve, in particular, the thought kept interfering with her celebrations. Nashida glanced at the clock built into the window of her city apartment. It was 11.11pm, forty-nine minutes until the holographic fireworks would begin over the bay to welcome in the new century.

'Maybe we should try now instead of the morning?' Nashida appealed to her husband, John.

'You're still a day away from being due for testing.'

'I want to try.'

'Okay. Let me get the stick.' John went to their bathroom and Nashida watched him return with a small device, which looked like a tube of lipstick. Nashida uncapped one end and placed the device against her fingertip. She pressed a button and barely felt the acupuncture thin needle prick her. A moment later the words they'd longed to see were displayed on an electronic panel: Pregnant: One to two weeks.

John smiled at Nashida and gave her a hug. 'Maybe this time?'

'Maybe.' Nashida smiled back; despite already losing three babies, the 'New Century' brought her a sense of hope.

'*Kairos* – the time is right,' she whispered to herself.

'We should call that new doctor in the morning and update him before our appointment next week,' John said.

'Yep. Hopefully, he can help us keep this one.'

#

Nashida and John knocked on the office door together. The fertility clinic was on the ground floor of St. Brigit's Hospital. They felt fortunate they'd made an appointment to see the fertility specialist six months ago, after their last miscarriage. Their self-driving car had dropped them off. While they'd been waiting for their appointment a message had appeared on John's watch to say the car had found a park seven minutes away.

'Come in,' a voice called. They opened the door and saw a tall, bearded man, who, in other circumstances, would have made an excellent stand-in for Santa Claus. His office was richly decorated with antique furniture and large gilded artworks. It was ostentatious yet tasteful.

'Hello, Mr and Mrs Jones. I'm Dr Hera. Welcome,' he said while reading their file.

'Hello, Doctor.' Nashida heard a quiver in her voice.

Dr Hera looked up from his notes.

'Sorry, Jasmine, I must have the wrong file. Wait, wrong part of the country.'

Nashida felt her face mirror the confusion on the doctor's.

'You're not Jasmine Didymus?'

'No. I'm Nashida Jones.'

'Do you have a twin?'

'No.'

'That's three times now,' Dr Hera muttered, 'Sorry, I thought you were someone else. How can I help you, Mrs Jones?'

'As you know, we're pregnant. This is our fourth pregnancy and we'd like to keep it. You were recommended to us, by our GP, Dr Smith.'

Dr Hera re-opened Nashida's file. Nashida could see the words multigravida and nulliparous next to the letters $M_3A_3$. She knew this meant her previous pregnancies had miscarried before the child was viable.

'Yes. Let me guess, all the previous ones miscarried at nine weeks.'

'Yes.'

'Just like Jasmine. Most bizarre.'

'What's special about nine weeks?' Nashida asked.

'Which for you would be the first of February.'

'We know,' said Nashida.

'Nothing in particular. Definitions vary, but it's just after a baby switches from being an embryo to a fetus.'

'So Doc, it seems odd that it would be so consistent,' John said.

'Exactly my thought, which is why I've been doing research into it. You two are not the first couple I've treated—'

The word 'treated' made Nashida's heart beat faster. '—with the same set of circumstances, good general health and a healthy uterus, sperm and eggs. In short there's no reason why you shouldn't be capable of having children.'

'So you can help us?' Nashida asked.

'I'm not sure how to say this. I've treated dozens of couples like yourselves and despite my best efforts, none were ever able to carry a baby past nine weeks.'

It didn't matter how gently the doctor had spoken, Nashida felt as though her heart had stopped beating.

She crossed her arms and slumped in her chair as tears started to run down her face. Nashida just wanted to be a mother. John placed an arm around her and gave her a gentle hug.

'I've started researching this and unlike my colleagues, I think it's wrong to blame the lifestyle of the parents. I'm convinced there's a genetic issue, which is why I've focussed my research on the embryo itself, at least what I can.'

'What have you found?' John asked as he absently stroked Nashida's back. Nashida sobbed quietly. Dr Hera looked at her with empathy.

'Only that it's odd that it's so similar in every pregnancy – always in the ninth week, right when the heart would be developing its four chambers. I'm guessing that something goes wrong and the fetus' heart stops. My theories are mostly theoretical since the Human Reproductive Tissue Act of 2063 prevents me from obtaining the aborted material to determine what went wrong… Looking at you now adds another piece to the puzzle. In nearly sixty years of practice, you're the third woman who has looked like another patient. And I'm not talking about a passing resemblance, I mean you are identical to a patient I had when I was in the country. Once or twice might be coincidence but three…'

'Doc, what can we do?' John asked.

'I'm afraid there isn't much. One of my previous

patients like you had the same thing happen nine times.'

'I won't give up,' said Nashida.

'We won't give up,' John gently corrected.

'Think about that. Nine times. Nine times of getting hopes up, the roller coaster of hormones and the strain on your relationship. As it was, two of those nine pregnancies were from different fathers. It doesn't seem to be an issue with the egg as since conception occurs readily. It's funny though, when I first started practicing, we were able to do all sorts of genetic testing, gender selection, pretty much designer baby stuff, but not since that damn Act came into effect.'

Nashida looked up. 'And that doesn't bother you?'

'Doing it or being stopped?'

'Both.' Nashida stopped crying but did not wipe the tears from her cheek. She thought the sight of them would encourage him to help her.

'I wish we could still do it. There was so much sense in having parents get a baby who was screened for genetic markers and was the gender the parents wanted. Those babies were so loved. I think in part due to the parents having a greater than usual sense of creation.'

Nashida heard the wistful tone she was hoping for.

'Well, Doctor, how about I let you experiment on me.'

John and Dr Hera's eyes widened.

'What do you mean?' Dr Hera said.

'How about you do an amniocentesis on me? You could then do some genetic testing on it.'

'Amnios aren't usually done until fourteen or fifteen weeks. You won't reach that gestation period. We could do CVS, which is chorionic villus sampling. That would give us cells from your baby that we could use.'

The word 'baby' made Nashida's heart skip another beat. This pregnancy she'd tried only to think of it as a bundle of cells.

'Please note that the procedure itself carries a risk of miscarriage… And it's illegal for me to perform.'

'Oh.' Nashida was crestfallen. She concentrated on clenching her feet to stop herself from breaking the silence. In her experience, if she gave a someone enough time in a situation like this, they'd break the silence and usually offer some measure of support.

'Did you know your parents?' Dr Hera asked after a pause.

'No. I have no recollection of my parents. I just remember starting school at four and being taken care of by my adoptive parents, nothing from before.'

'See, now that's odd. My previous patient said almost the same thing. Most people have images or some foggy memories from the age of three. But you and your doppelganger, not so much. Both of you were adopted, neither remember your biological parents or early childhood and you are both incapable of carrying a child past nine weeks gestation.'

The finality implicit in the doctor's last sentence caused Nashida to wince. She felt John give her another squeeze.

'Yet all of those things are why I want to be a mother. I want to be there for someone like no one was for me, I want to bring a child into this world and nurture it. I want it to be my child…'

'And they are also reasons why my curiosity is piqued. I mean three pairings like yours are not just a coincidence.' Dr Hera leaned forward. 'A hundred and thirty odd years ago a researcher deliberately separated identical twins who'd been given up for adoption and secretly studied them. The details of his study, which were only released in 2066, were so controversial that he didn't want the public to see them until at least half a century after he'd died. I'm just thinking aloud, but what if you're part of some similar kind of study?'

Nashida felt herself not wanting to think about such a thing but knew this was how she'd get the support she needed to find out more about why she couldn't have children. What if someone had done this to her?

Nashida nodded. 'It's possible. I guess I'll have to investigate that notion somehow. So, would you be willing to do a CVS on me?'

'Only because there's something going on that I can't explain. But if we do this then there would need to be conditions, since you're asking me to break the law and risk not only my registration but also a hefty fine.'

'What are the conditions?' John asked. Nashida found herself willing to agree to anything.

'Firstly, you have to see this through.'

'Don't worry, Nashida is one of the most determined people you'll meet. It's part of the reason I fell in love with her. She isn't afraid of chasing the bigger picture, the bigger understanding...'

Nashida reached up and squeezed John's hand. 'Thanks, Hun.'

'Secondly, I will treat you like a normal patient. The paper trail and invoicing will show that you are receiving fertility treatment. You'll follow a normal appointment and payment schedule for one of my patients.'

Nashida and John nodded.

'Thirdly, you tell no one about this. No friends, family or anyone. Discuss it between you two, but no one else,' more nodding, 'Finally, any investigation that you make cannot lead back to me. No references to me are to be written anywhere, no notes about your 'doctor'; nothing. I'll do a few tests to help you but that's all. I may be willing to risk my registration since I'm close to retirement, but I'll be damned if I let it be thrown away.'

'Yes,' they both replied.

'One more thing. You'll let me know the outcome of anything you find.'

They both nodded.

'You should probably start by looking into the national fertility rate, something about that has been bugging me but I've never been able to put my finger on what exactly is wrong with it.'

'But that's been steady,' said Nashida.

'That's what our state's statistics say, but they only give us a figure, not the numbers behind how it was calculated. My colleagues and I have only ever experienced increasing demand for our services, despite a surge in the number of doctors taking up our specialty. I'm wondering if there isn't a Simpson's paradox at play.'

'Huh?' John said.

'It's a statistical thing where if you combine sets of data that show a particular correlation and then recalculate the relationship, you wind up with either the nullification or reversal of the correlation you thought existed. It's bothered me for a while. If you ask for more details as someone who's trying to make sense of her miscarriages, you might get a different response to me; maybe find a sympathetic ear.'

'Okay,' John said.

'Oh, and remember that I've never been able to help any of my patients like you. This may give some answers as to why, but that's all.'

Nashida felt tears well again as she and John stood, thanked the doctor and pressed the button for their car to come and collect them.

#

After a late night talking through permutations and possibilities, Nashida was reminded why she'd fallen in love with John; despite him trying to be the voice of reason and saying that the idea of a conspiracy was far-fetched, she'd awoken to a cooked breakfast, a written plan of how to start her investigation and note saying he'd called in sick on her behalf.

Nashida's first task was to write to each state's Minister for Health and look up and include each state's fertility rate in her messages to them. She'd assumed it would be given as a figure of births per thousand women, but was surprised to find that it was simply a value of births per woman. As she researched she found that worldwide the birth rate was over five children per woman in the 1960s, 2.451 in 2015 and 1.3 in 2098. The states provided the data for the last decade. The value was unchanging amongst all of them – always 1.3. This bugged Nashida. It was only after she'd written her messages to the Ministers for Health and had the satisfaction of putting a line through an item on her 'to do' list, that she realised why. The earlier statistics were given to three decimal places, but the recent ones only had one. This could conceal a decline in the rate, and that could mean that the idea of a conspiracy was not so fanciful after all.

Researching and wording her messages so that they wouldn't raise concerns had taken Nashida all morning, so she was surprised when she received her first reply within an hour. It read:

*Dear Nashida Jones,*

*Thank you for your message about fertility rates in our state. You note that the rate has changed compared to historical values. This is true and due to cultural shifts in modern society compared to a hundred years ago. As you are probably aware, the average age a woman has her first child now is thirty-seven and this is over fifteen years later than the equivalent age in the 1960s when the birth rate was over five children per woman. As a woman's fertility naturally declines with age, the fact that our birth rate is constant, despite an increasing average age for having the first child implies an increase in fertility. Similarly, families are having fewer children. The mean value is 1.3 children, but the mode and median value are a single child. Most families are choosing to stop at one. As you know our country, as part of the United Countries Partnership, has chosen not to place limits on the number of children you can have, unlike some non-member nations. Additionally, the more recent statistics are an anomaly – the rate of births per woman has actually been increasing amongst those who want children, we've just had fewer women of childbearing age choose to reproduce. We thank you for your interest in this matter.*

The message was signed off with 'Warm Regards' and the Minister's name. It seemed like a particularly quick reply. The second read through made Nashida realise that no specific information from her message was referred to, and that it was just a form letter. Why would they have a form letter for what must be an uncommon request?

Her concern increased when an almost identically worded response from another minister arrived ten minutes later. By the time she'd received a third reply within an hour and a half, her suspicions were well and truly raised. The third response at least had a different opening line: 'Thank you for raising your concerns, this troubled me too.' The remainder of the form letter was the same, but the sign off had an offer for her to "please get in touch if you have any further queries".

By the time John arrived home, Nashida had received five replies. After he'd read them all he sat with Nashida and handed her a glass of orange juice. They sat at their square dining table on adjacent corners.

Nashida sipped her juice. 'So what do you think? Am I paranoid?'

'You know I'm trying to be the reasonable one, but I must admit, I'm being swayed. You might be onto something.'

'Thanks, Hun. I'm a bit stuck on what to do next though.'

'What have you ticked off from the list?'

'Sent the messages to the ministers, lodged an information request with the national library for articles relating to fertility from the last fifty years and read more about fertility and pregnancy than is healthy. I mean the more you know about what can go wrong…it's a miracle how many healthy babies are born. That's everything on the list.'

'Oh, so you're losing interest?'

She smiled. 'What do you mean? I mean come on Hun, you've met me. Of course, I'm not.'

'So why haven't you replied to the minister from WA?'

'Huh?'

'Read the message again and remove the form letter. It basically says this concerns me please get in touch.'

Nashida looked at the message again.

'You're right!'

John grinned. 'Don't be so surprised. You may have married me for my looks, but I have a brain as well.' Nashida laughed. 'I think it was the other way round.'

'Anyway, you've done well today and now you have two things to do tomorrow: wait for the library to reply and contact that minister. So, now that's established, can we watch the next episode of our show, once you've called in sick again for tomorrow?'

Nashida nodded and gave the voice command for the Holovisual display to start the next episode. The windows became opaque, leaving only the clock visible. Nashida and John sat on the couch and watched the action appearing right in front of them.

#

John had left for work before Nashida checked her messages. There were two. The first was from her boss saying he hoped she was okay and would be back at work soon. The other was from the National Library. They had replied to her request and sent her a login that would give her access to a petabyte of data. The data had been copied onto the library member server for her to access over the next fortnight. She sent a quick message to the minister asking him to call, before starting to sort through the massive amount of information using a mixture of voice and gesture based commands. Her local device projected basic information holographically and drew detail from the server as required.

Nashida felt like she was moving through the information, even though she was seated. Images flew past her as she filtered files. The archive was comprehensive and contained local news, academic articles, medical articles, documentaries; even movies that had childbirth as a theme. The volume of data was overwhelming her and the conspiracy theorist inside said that was intentional, so she spoke the words that throughout her life she'd used to calm down, 'I am the seeker. I will find what I need.' Years of conditioning kicked in and she felt herself regain focus. A few searches and swipes later, she discovered an article entitled 'What is happening in our country towns?' It was a forty-one-year-old editorial from a rural paper called *The Northam Monthly*.

### *What is Happening in Our Country Towns?*

*The Northam Monthly has noticed an alarming trend within Northam and many of our neighbouring towns. It seems there has been a rise in what the government are calling 'regional centres'. These mini-cities are like black holes absorbing all the small towns around them. What surprises us is how blatant the government is about wanting people to move to these centres. They stack them with resources, which are then discontinued from the towns. This applies, in particular, to medicine and education, as doctors and teachers from small towns are being offered huge incentives to move to such places. The sad outcome is these crucial services leave the communities they've previously served. There has been an alarming increase in the need for reproductive services in our town over the last decade and we know of at least a dozen couples who've moved to such a centre in order to be able to access such services. We hereby call on our community to write to the government and implore them to reverse their support for regional centres and restore services to rural communities before our way of life is eroded and made unsustainable.*

There was a tag at the bottom of the image indicating a related article. Nashida selected it. The following month's letters page from the same paper appeared. Nashida gasped as she read it; the editors from seven other community papers had written in stating they'd also noticed the same push to regional centres and that fertility treatment seemed to be a focus. Nashida searched for city based news articles from the same timeframe, but found none in the database. It seemed this started as a regional problem.

The more she thought about it the more questions the discovery posed. Why would reproduction only be affected in country towns— the places where you'd expect people to have larger families? Why would the phenomenon occur in multiple towns that were geographically isolated from each other? A new search for similar stories from only regional news sources found another two articles, one of which also mentioned decreasing fertility in the township as a specific cause of why the town was dying. Nashida searched for the fertility rates of specific rural towns but found that such data was not available. She took a breath, reminded herself that she would find what she needed and realised she could look up population growth instead. She found that the population trend line seemed to be heading upwards in 2050. Yet, over the last few decades, it had gone negative in all cases, bar one where the line had flattened. In comparison, the cities rates had been slightly upwards, probably due to the influx from the death of the rural towns.

Another hour of searching proved less productive, although she was able to find list of country towns and the year they were abandoned. The first township was vacated in 2060 and by the year 2090, fifty-seven places had become ghost towns, including the one she'd called home until the age of eight.

The visual information in front of her was suddenly replaced by a yellow symbol. Pressing it opened the call she'd been waiting for. The hologram of her caller was of an older gentleman, with a shaved head and bright hazel eyes. His suit was lime green. He seemed full of energy.

'Hello Nashida, my name is Graham Mendax. You wrote to me yesterday and asked me to give you a call. How can I be of service?'

'Hi Graham, thanks for getting back to me. I'm interested in why the fertility rate is declining.'

'Sorry for interrupting, but that isn't true. It's actually increasing as I wrote in my message to you yesterday.'

'Yes you gave your reasons why, but I'm not sure they add up.'

'They do.'

'Well anyway, I'm interested about how the birth rate seems to be going down regionally, but up in cities.'

Graham's eyes widened in shock.

'That's not something I'm aware of, so I'm afraid I won't be able to help you. As always, if you're ever near my office, call in for a chat. I'm always in on Wednesdays. It's good for politicians to have a chance to meet constituents.' Graham disconnected the call. Immediately, the files returned.

Nashida took a few deep breaths to calm her nerves, and then remembered John's words of yesterday. Take away the 'company line' and what was left was an invite to meet with him in person, on a Wednesday. *Tomorrow.* Looking up his offices was straightforward as the information was stored when he called. Nashida pressed on the address in the holographic display and then gave a voice command, 'Book flights and car to get me here tomorrow morning and back tomorrow night.' A moment later a confirmation of her flights appeared.

Nashida browsed the files some more, but her intent was blunted by the progress she'd already made. With a sigh, she stopped and had her drinks machine make her an espresso. As she sipped the richly flavoured coffee, her mind wandered to her first miscarriage. They'd known she was pregnant for a month and had decided to share the news with her adoptive parents and John's parents since it was Fathers Day. It seemed a fitting date to let them know they'd be grandparents. Together, they'd told them all at a special breakfast. Nashida had noticed a switch in John that morning, even before they'd shared the news. Later, he confided it was the first time he'd really imagined being a father and the thought that in a year's time he'd be celebrating as a father and not just a son really excited him. It was that afternoon that the first spots of blood had appeared. 'It's probably nothing,' she'd reassured John. But by the evening the blood was appearing as drops. A call to Nashida's doctor and then a visit to the maternity hospital confirmed her worst fears. She was having a miscarriage. They spent the night in the hospital and were discharged in the morning. John was horrified to learn that a miscarriage might last five or six days. He'd always had the understanding that since you gave birth in a day, a miscarriage would take as long. Nashida had noticed how much he'd been affected by this revelation and how attentive he'd been while the process continued. I'm lucky to have him, she'd thought.

Having to tell their parents, who'd been so excited by the news, was gut wrenching. Nashida recalled the numbness in her voice as she told them. She regretted disconnecting the call so quickly, but she couldn't look at them. The second miscarriage hadn't been much easier, other than knowing what to do, there was still a profound sense of loss even though they'd kept the pregnancy to themselves. By the third, they knew the routine. It still wasn't easy but was almost expected. John had been a rock throughout each pregnancy, despite the emotional roller coaster each month they tried to get pregnant. Nashida knew her hormone shifts hadn't helped either.

John arrived home a few hours later. Nashida gave

him a long hug when he walked in. 'I love you,' she said. After talking about what she'd discovered and her flying interstate the next day, they watched another episode of their show. It was a welcome distraction.

#

Arriving in the western city brought regret that she'd neglected to bring sunglasses. The city was much closer to the equator than where she lived. Nashida had been here a number of times and always appreciated the outdoor lifestyle and vibrancy of the city. She particularly liked that the flight was only an hour, meaning that due to a two-hour time difference she arrived before she left.

The car took her straight to the minister's offices, which were in a northern suburb of the city. She walked through the triple glazed doors and into a space that was clearly not meant to be functioning as a reception area. There was a bench seat, but no obvious place for reporting to. Nashida cleared her throat. At once a young woman's head popped up from behind a partition.

'Can I help you?'

'Hi, I'd like to speak to Graham please?'

'Certainly. Who shall I say is asking for him?'

'Nashida Jones.'

'And what is it about?'

The question stumped her for a moment, 'Uh, I'm a

constituent and it's a local matter.'

'He likes those. I'll just go and get him.'

A moment later she returned with Graham, who looked the same as his hologram, except this time his suit was sky blue.

'Nashida was it?' he asked politely.

'Yes.'

'Please come this way.' He led her through a maze of partitions to a private office. He shut the door behind them and invited her to take a seat opposite him at his jarrah desk.

'What was it you'd like to discuss?' he asked in the same energetic and friendly tone of their call. He took out a stick of chewing gum, unwrapped it and started chewing. Nashida found this annoying. After explaining the purpose of the visit and the desire for more information, she was surprised when he said 'I understand your concerns and that this is something that is personal for you. Unfortunately though, there's nothing more I can add. The reported statistics don't match what you're saying and your idea that fertility specialists are swamped is easily explained by the increase in the standard of living that's occurred in the last few decades. Putting it simply, more people can afford such health care, so more people are seeking it.'

Nashida felt betrayed. She glared at Graham, so incensed she couldn't bring herself to speak. Her anger intensified as he guided her to the door and said, 'Thank you for coming in. It's always nice to meet a constituent. Would you mind putting this in the bin outside for me?' He passed her his gum wrapper. Nashida nodded mutely, absently put the wrapper in her jacket pocket and allowed herself to be led out of the building. She wandered over to a nearby bench, sat down, put her head in her hands and sobbed uncontrollably. Damn hormones. What was she meant to do now? Nashida couldn't believe she'd found out so much yet felt so powerless to do anything with what she knew.

She pushed the button for her car to collect her. The trip to the airport took twenty minutes, during which she called John to let him know the trip was for nought. He asked if something hadn't been said to help her, since he'd convinced himself Graham really wanted to help and would when they'd been able to talk quietly in person.

'No, he was a condescending jerk,' she replied.

Nashida spent the flight trying to think of another path to take in her investigation. She was the seeker. She would find what she needed. Maybe she could visit one of the ghost towns or track down some of the editors who'd written the opinion pieces? Her instinct told her that while such things were feasible, they would be fruitless. She resigned herself to the fact that her journey had reached a dead end. This annoyed her, as she was sure this was something that had been done to her. Maybe Dr Hera would be able to find out more about the mechanics of what caused the miscarriages, even though that wouldn't tell her why she'd been chosen to suffer them.

#

On Friday, two weeks later, Nashida and John went to Dr Hera for what would be billed as a routine first-trimester scan. In reality, they were there for the chorionic villus sampling. Dr Hera rubbed a local anaesthetic on Nashida's belly as she lay on the examining table in the doctor's office. He had to ask John to hold the ultrasound in place while he did the procedure, as they couldn't risk anyone else being present. Dr Hera took a long needle and explained that under the guidance of the ultrasound he would insert it through her abdomen and into her uterus. He would then direct it to her placenta and take a sample of cells. These cells would be cultured for ten days and analysed— something Dr Hera would do as sending the sample off for analysis would not match the billing codes they'd use. Getting time in a lab to perform the study was straightforward. The local university encouraged people to book in and use their facilities over the summer break as long as they gave partial credit to the university for any publishable findings.

As the needle penetrated through the layers of her

abdomen, Nashida gasped.

'Does it hurt?' John asked with concern.

'No, it just feels extremely uncomfortable.'

Dr Hera looked at the ultrasound. 'Hmm, it looks like there is some calcification going on. We'll have to look for that in the test results.'

A minute later and the cells had been collected. Dr Hera placed a bandage over the puncture wound. He carefully emptied the syringe into a specimen tube, as John helped Nashida off the table and hugged.

'I'm sure you've already worked this out, but we won't get the results of this until after next week - your ninth week,' Dr Hera said.

'I know,' Nashida said. 'Thank you. I guess we'll see you again when the miscarry begins then.'

#

Nashida and John had spent Saturday talking about what more they could do and what it would mean if they couldn't have children. They intermittently watched their show when the conversation got too raw. On Sunday morning, John suggested going for a walk to clear their heads.

'I'll just grab a jacket,' Nashida said, heading to the cupboard and grabbing the first one she saw.

John tossed her the car button, which also doubled as their front door key. Nashida put it in her pocket and felt something she wasn't expecting. She pulled out a gum wrapper and looked at it in puzzlement before she remembered where it had come from. She was about to angrily rip it into tiny pieces when she noticed writing on it. There was a doodle of a camera and the word 'sorry' as well as a name: Mark Doleo.

A search revealed a former federal minister with that name. He'd been in charge of the nation's Future Fund and Healthcare. A few more searches revealed he was due to speak at a nearby fundraiser luncheon the next day, February 1st. Nashida immediately booked a ticket to the event, despite the very high cost and her lack of support for the political party. She was free due to her expected miscarriage, which meant she'd already arranged to work from home for the next week. During her walk she made a mental note to make up some hours in the evening.

#

The venue for the talk was an upmarket restaurant. Nashida ate her way through the seven-course degustation without appreciating the food or worrying about following the rules for eating while pregnant. At last, the time came for Mark to make his speech.

'I am a hundred and four years old and have memories that span three centuries. I know I only have five or six years left to live and so, as I near the end of my life, I've spent some time reflecting on a life well lived and this is the theme of my talk today. I'll start with the triumphs, move onto the regrets and finish with the lessons I've learnt.'

Nashida hadn't planned on paying attention to the talk, but she was captivated by how he described life at the start of the previous century. His reference to being a millennial took her a moment to understand and his discussion of what was new technology then but ancient now fascinated Nashida. Mark moved on to his career in politics where he'd risen through the ranks until he became the Future Fund and Healthcare Minister. He listed the progress his ministry had made in getting people to move to regional centres, thereby getting them better access to health care, while reducing the cost of services as a major achievement. He highlighted how increases in the speed of transport meant that such centres mitigated the need to build infrastructure in the towns and that people could commute to farming and related jobs from the new hubs. For a centenarian, Mark seemed alert and well spoken. She was reminded that he'd only retired a decade ago, choosing to work well past the age his contemporaries had stopped.

'I was so proud of what we were able to do and of being part of the process that streamlined services to our nation and helped us develop the modern way of living…'

Nashida shuddered at the thought of country towns being killed.

'… that it may surprise some of you to learn that this is where my talk shifts to the regrets I have.'

Like many in the room, Nashida did a double take. 'We thought what we were doing was a humane way to improve society, and it certainly was compared to how other countries approached the same issue. However, I can't help but wonder about the impact of losing all our small towns to regional sub-cities or about the impact on the people who had to move. They had a way of life that's gone now and I regret being part of that process.'

Nashida's mind reeled. Had he just made an allusion to a program she'd been affected by?

Although she had some idea that the government had such a desire, to hear first-hand that there had been a deliberate policy for such push towards the regional cities was a shock.

After the talk, Nashida joined the queue to say hello to Mark. While she was waiting she felt a familiar sensation between her legs. And so it begins, she thought, refusing to let the moisture welling in her eyes turn into tears. A moment later, she was face to face with her last lead.

'Hello, Mark. My name is Nashida Jones and I believe you can give me some answers.'

'Certainly – to what questions though?'

'Why I can't have children.'

'What do you mean?'

His expression seemed concerned, which for some reason infuriated her. Nashida felt rage and a surge of hormones build inside. She put her hand down her pants, then shoved her bloody finger in front of his face.

'This. This is what I mean. I'm nine weeks pregnant and miscarrying as we speak,' she hissed.

The shock on Mark's face was plain to see, but could she see guilt as well? Nashida tried to ignore the few people who'd shown interest in the scene she was creating.

'I'm so sorry to hear that. Why don't you hang around for a bit and once I've greeted these people we can talk a little more privately?'

His tone remained calm and Nashida found his logic hard to fault, so after a nod, she headed to the bathroom to deal with her bleeding.

She called John and gave him an update on what was happening to and with her. He was sympathetic and sounded sad, despite anticipating the events. 'Wish I was there to support you.'

'Thanks Hun, it's okay. I know you're needed there today.'

Nashida returned to her table. It took forty-five minutes for people to clear enough for Mark join her.

'Thank you for waiting. Shall we sit outside? My legs are tired after all this standing and I could use some fresh air.'

He motioned for her to follow him out to a small balcony which overlooked the city. As Nashida sat she mused that this would be a marvellous place to sit and sip a coffee. The view of the city with its greys and glassed buildings was complemented by the blue of the ocean and the green of the wide grass strip that set the city back from the water.

'You are stunningly beautiful.'

The compliment caught Nashida by surprise.

'Uh, thank you. Huh?'

'There's a reason for that. Have you ever wondered why you can't remember anything before the age of four?'

Nashida felt her jaw opening, but no words came out.

'Before I get to that, I suppose I should confirm a few things. You can't remember anything before the age of four, you miscarry at nine weeks and you were adopted and raised in the country, probably in what is now a ghost town.'

'Yes.'

'Interesting. Since you approached me an hour ago, I've hardly been able to converse with anyone, such was my curiosity. You are the first to track me down. If I may ask, how did you piece it together? Did you meet a twin? We tried to have controls so that wouldn't happen.'

'No a doctor had met three sets of doppelgangers after shifting cities, and each of them miscarried at nine weeks.'

'Ah.' The gleam in Mark's eyes was unmistakeable.

'We didn't anticipate the consequence of doctors moving cities… I suppose that rather than immediately confessing all, I should ask what you hope to gain from approaching me? I can provide some answers, but if you want revenge or justice, you won't find it here. We had approval. The worst you could do is cause a modicum of embarrassment for the government, which would never go further as the issue would not be reported in the official media. Besides, if you tried to spread the message, no one would believe you.'

'I have to know why I can't have kids and what hope there might be to change that. I want answers about why I'm the way I am.'

'There is no hope, so if that's all you want you might as well leave now. Answers though, I will provide. Ask away.'

Nashida froze. She'd never really extinguished hop that something could be done. The idea that despite coming this far she would be unable to have a baby was too overwhelming for her to contemplate.

'Why can't I remember anything before the age of four?'

'You're a clone.'

Nashida felt like her chair was no longer supporting her.

'In the 2030s the world's population reached nine billion people. This was more than had been anticipated just fifteen years earlier. Governments around the world realised that without intervention we'd reach the carrying capacity of the earth before, well, this year. This would mean some form of catastrophic event would be likely, with what we described as 'indiscriminate outcomes' meaning no one could control who'd live or die. This was unacceptable. Many countries introduced strict birth control, or deliberately poisoned a proportion of their people.'

Nashida gasped as she remembered the stories of the mass poisonings in Atlasantia in the 2050s.

'We created a more humane way of controlling the population. It was simple. We cloned women who were deemed highly desirable due to their personality and background, and altered their DNA so they'd always miscarry. The physical attractiveness of the clones was not only due to selection, but the cloning process, where tight controls meant they developed a highly symmetrical appearance.'

'Why not men?' Nashida asked through gritted teeth.

'It was nothing to do with sexism, I can assure you. The simple truth is that women were chosen due to their genetic superiority, not having one of those peskily weak Y chromosomes, and the success ratio of functioning clone to failure was much better with women. The gene we changed was on the X chromosome and inserting the corrupted gene on both X chromosomes guaranteed it would be passed on, and prevent any offspring being born. If we tried that with men they'd still be able to have sons.'

Nashida tried to gather her thoughts as Mark paused for a moment.

'Sending the clones to rural towns rather than cities was my idea, and at the time I was quite proud of it. Over time, it meant the birth rate would drop below the death rate in those towns. This fit in with the government's desire for the towns to be absorbed to make sub-cities where resources and infrastructure could be concentrated.'

'How many like me are there?'

'We sent out about forty thousand clones, paid for by appropriating money from the future fund, which I controlled. Some were adopted into target towns, while others were raised in a city and then made an offer they couldn't refuse to get them to move to a target town. We did this before they reached their thirties and started wanting babies.'

'So err… I mean… How? How could you think that was humane?'

'We didn't need to cull any humans or use force to stop people having children. Desirability of the clones was not based on looks alone but range of factors including personality, intelligence, compassion and health. The men who married such women got a great partner.'

Mark's face was full of pride and Nashida had the impression he'd long been wanting to share the breadth of his plan with someone and have it recognised for its genius.

'But what about the clones and their feelings? All I want is to be a mother and you've stolen that from me. How can you not think that's cruel? How can you think that doing that is not inhuman, let alone inhumane?'

Mark's face dropped and his voice cracked. 'That's true. We tended to think of the clones as a means to an end and not as people. The impact on them is something we should've thought about and something I've recently been reflecting on. We were too caught up in what we were trying to achieve to stop and consider the consequences for those involved. For that, I am very sorry.'

Nashida grunted, annoyed that she found the apology sincere.

'The beauty of the plan for us was that the clones would die after having served their purpose meaning that the impact of what we'd done could be controlled. I mean, the alternative such as introducing a gene, like a recessive one, that would have had more random implementation and longer term consequences which could have been disastrous. We'd have no off switch. As it stands this program was able to be stopped in 2080.'

Nashida realised that was when she was fifteen.

'What can be done to fix me?'

'I told you before. You can't be helped. The gene is active in the follicles in your ovaries. You'd have to knock out the gene in the ripening egg. That's totally illegal. The Act of 2063 prohibits it. That's why I told you there's no hope. You'd be hard pressed to find someone who'd know how to help you these days anyway.'

For the second time that day Nashida summoned all her willpower to prevent her from crying.

'What else would you like to know?'

'Can I get in touch with you again?'

'I suppose so. Here are my details.' He touched his device and made a flicking gesture. Nashida felt a vibration in her pocket.

'One more thing. Did you ever think about the babies?'

'What do you mean?'

'They have a life too, however brief it is. They have a brain and a heart when they die.'

Nashida watched Mark's face contort in what she presumed was horror from considering the thought for the first time.

#

The next day Nashida went with John to see Dr Hera. He greeted her with an expectant look.

'Yes Doc, I'm miscarrying.'

He nodded.

Nashida spent a few minutes sharing what she'd learnt.

'Your information confirms what the ultrasound and CVS revealed. The fetus' heart was calcified.'

'So it died from a broken heart. I feel like mine is heading that way too,' Nashida said. John reached for her hand.

'Hmm.' Clearly, an idea had occurred to the doctor. 'Can you come back in a week? I'll need to confirm that the miscarriage is complete anyway.'

#

A week later, they assembled in the doctor's office once again. Dr Hera beamed as he welcomed them.

'What's got you all excited, Doc?' John asked.

The doctor directed his reply to Nashida.

'You mentioned the fault preventing development was on the X chromosome and I knew its effect. With some research, I was able to identify the specific gene. It's called CXorf63k. It tells the heart cells to actively take up calcium until they no longer function. If I can extract an egg from you I think I can use the old CRISPRZ protocol to remove it.'

'Are you trying to say…'

'Yes, I think I have a way to help you carry a baby to term.'

'Is that legal? I don't want to get too excited and be crushed again,' John said quietly. Nashida looked up at him and realised she often overlooked how much he wanted a child as well.

'I thought the minister said no one knew how to undo the change,' John said.

'Yes, it's illegal. Has been since 2063, but I've been practicing since well before then, so I used to do it regularly. Admittedly, it's been nearly forty years so I'm rusty and will have to launch a study on rats or something that will enable me to order the materials, but I think it can be done.'

'Could helping me draw attention to you?' Nashida asked.

'It's nice of you to be so compassionate. I think it's a calculated risk. The only concern might be the extent to which the government is still tracking you. If we're successful and you do have a baby that might raise a flag which could cause a lot of trouble.'

'I'll ask Mark,' Nashida said.

She moved to the side of the office so the others couldn't be seen when she called. A short conversation revealed that since the program had ended in 2080 the monitoring of the clones had ceased as it wasn't deemed necessary to move them around anymore.

'Why do you ask?' he queried.

'Just wanting to know how free I am,' Nashida said as she disconnected the call.

#

On December 24th Nashida answered a call from Dr Hera.

'Hello, Nashida and John. I just wanted to call and say congratulations on reaching the second trimester. You deserve it.'

'Thank you,' they said in unison.

'This means you can tell people now,' Dr Hera said, the smile evident in his voice as well as his face.

When he disconnected, Nashida and John grinned at each other. Nashida could tell they were both thinking the same thing; our parents are going to love this Christmas present.

# The Legend of Legend

The lounge room was located in the penthouse of Ivory Towers. It had an old world vibe; wood panels lined the lower half of the walls, artwork dominated the rest. A gas fireplace added warmth and character, and two sling chairs were oriented to it rather than the view through the full-length windows. Some whisky added a level of comfort and focus that encouraged philosophical conversation.

'Did you know you can make anything sound awesome just by adding the words 'of legend' after it?' Michael Episteme asked his friend.

Carl Engels leaned forward for his glass.

'Hmm… The snot … of legend. The cancer … of legend. The legend … of legend. Yep, seems to hold true.'

Michael smiled. 'The legend of legend; that was a good story.'

'What do you mean?'

'Well, you know the legend of legend. The whole Egg of Truth thing.'

Carl frowned.

'You don't know it?' Michael teased.

'I'm not sure,' Carl said softly.

'Can't bring yourself to say no?' Michael smirked. Carl waved his hand dismissively and pointed to his friend's glass.

'Just take a sip of your whisky and tell me what you know.'

'Okay. The legend of legend tells of a kidney shaped egg that when opened reveals some universal truth.'

'Kidney shaped egg?'

'Yes, that always struck me as odd, but you're interrupting,' Michael said.

'My apologies, go on.'

'One telling of the story has it coming out of Prussia at the end of the nineteenth century and disappearing after being seen in Switzerland. Another has it as belonging to some English princess; she didn't know its value and gave it to her aunt.'

'Interesting and quite a puzzle. I've always found that if you get stuck with the answer to a problem, question the assumptions of the answer. You say you found the reference to it being kidney shaped odd.'

'Yes'

'Why?' Carl asked.

'Because, who's ever heard of a kidney shaped egg?'

'So that's our first issue. What else?'

'The whole Prussia thing is strange, particularly if you take the approach as I do that the two parts of the legend are true.'

'So what else could it be?'

'I don't know, England had already shored up relationships with the Prussians. A gift like that would be unnecessary.'

'What about Chinese whispers? I mean Prussia and Russia sound similar,' Carl suggested.

'Yeah, as a kid I always thought they were the same place.'

'And if you take Russia and egg what do you get?'

'Faberge,' Michael said without hesitation.

'Exactly. Plus, their eggs were known to have 'surprises' in them.'

'And they started making them at the right time for the legend.'

'Just to add to the mix, the Faberges went to Switzerland after leaving Russia during the revolution.'

'Hmm … I have a vague recollection that the Tsar of Russia married an English Princess.'

Michael took out his smartphone.

'While you're looking that up, I'll get us another round.' Carl walked to his bookcase and at the press of a hidden button a section of it swung open, revealing a liquor cabinet. 'Same again?' Carl queried.

'How about something a bit peatier?'

'The Phenolmore it is then.'

Carl handed Michael his drink and looked at him expectantly.

Michael looked up from his phone. 'I've discovered that before he became the Tsar of Russia, a kid named Nicholas fell in love with his English cousin. She was half English, half German… technically German, not English like I thought. Five years after they'd last met and after a series of letters, he met her again at the wedding of their mutual cousins, and he proposed. She turned him down. Apparently, something changed her mind and when he tried again the next day she said yes.'

'Do you think the egg could've been a gift to her that changed her mind?'

'It would certainly fit. I mean she goes from no to yes within a day. Something pretty profound must have occurred.'

'It could have been her family, but okay. What else?'

'The year was 1894. Nine years after the first official

Imperial Faberge egg was made.'

'What if the egg was meant to be his gift to the bride and groom and knowing its significance he instead gave it to the woman he loved, to show how much she meant to him.'

'Makes sense,' Michael said.

'Yes, but we'll never know.'

'Indeed.'

'What are we looking for then?'

'It would also be wrong to look for something too ornate. The first eggs were much humbler than the later ones.'

'So we'd be looking for a simple egg that may have been a prototype Imperial Egg. Which brings us back to your original concern, none of the imperial eggs are kidney shaped. How do we solve that conflict?'

'You're a bioengineer, so you must know a lot of biology. What do you know about kidneys? Maybe there will be a clue there?'

'They filter your blood and produce urine. They do this through ultrafiltration, active transport and osmosis.'

Michael's eyes started glazing over.

'They're part of the renal system and their basic unit is the nephron which is made up of the glomerulus, proximal convoluted tubule…'

Michael's head twitched. 'What did you say about

nephrite?'

'I didn't. I said nephron. What's nephrite?'

'My wife has a thing for geology and collects minerals. Her favourite is jade.'

'So?'

'She's taught me jade is the name given to two different minerals: jadeite and nephrite. If we take this whole Chinese whispers approach again, what if someone heard nephrite, mistakenly associated it with kidneys and then when they told the legend added that it was kidney shaped.'

'Sounds feasible.'

'And since nephrite is a dark green colour, we would then be looking for a dark green egg, similar but less ornate than later Faberge eggs, maybe bearing the Faberge mark, whose provenance could be traced back to England in the 1890s.'

'Have we solved a hundred year old mystery just by sitting in our armchairs?'

'Don't forget the whisky. I'm sure that helped too, but maybe.'

'Now what?' Carl said.

'I guess we try to track down such an egg.'

Michael started searching on his phone, while Carl used his laptop.

'Hmph,' Carl said.

'What?'

'There appears to be a real Faberge egg that's made of nephrite. It's called the pansy egg and its surprise is a heart containing miniature portraits of the Russian Tsar's family.'

'Did you know the pansy used to be a symbol of freethinking?'

'No, but I'll try to remember that.'

They resumed their search. After half an hour Carl said, 'Did we really think we'd be able to find it online?'

'I guess not. So what do we do?'

'I have a friend in England. She's on speaking terms with the royals. The rumour is she'll be made a Dame soon. I'll give her a call and see if she can help. Maybe ask a few questions?'

'Sounds like a plan. It's getting late, so it's probably time to call it a night. Thank you for a most entertaining evening.'

'Indeed. Goodnight, Michael,' Carl said as he saw Michael from his home.

#

Two days later, Michael answered his phone.

'Good morning, Michael, how are you?' Carl asked.

'Well. You?'

'Fine. I got in touch with my friend Rachel. She said she would have a quiet word with the Prince next time she saw him, to see if anyone in the family can remember the egg we're looking for. She also made a suggestion to try the UK and European auction houses. She's going to send through a bunch of their catalogues. Should be a good place to start.'

'Agreed. What now?'

'Keep searching and hope something turns up. Remember we're basing this on shaky logic and we can't really say that our alcohol infused flight of fancy was anything more than that.'

'Agreed.'

'So we may not find anything,' Carl said.

'Which would be a shame.'

'But still, it does seem to fit quite neatly doesn't it?'

'Absolutely.'

'So we're not giving up?'

'I guess not.'

'Excellent. See you soon my friend.'

#

Seven months later Carl's phone rang at 3.13am. He answered it sleepily.

'Carl, it's Michael. I've found it.'

'Found what?'

'The legend of legend.'

Carl sat up as though cold water had been poured over him. His eyes dilated and his chest started thumping.

'Where? How?'

'Smithee's Auctions. They're near Lancaster in

England. They have an auction next month and the egg is in their catalogue.'

'How can you be sure?'

'Intuition, a perfectly valid way of knowing by the way, and the description. Item number 017 in lot 313. Jade egg circa 1900 in the style of Faberge (replica). Unknown origin. Sold on behalf of the Moritz family. Estimated range £30 – 35K. After reading the description I researched the seller and found out that they're famous art collectors, but that's not the best bit…'

'Stop pausing for effect and tell me,' Carl said.

'You remember the wedding that Nicholas went to where we think he gave the egg to his cousin?'

'Whom he married.'

'Yes. Well, the Moritz family were adopted into that family in the 60s.'

'So we have a plausible connection.'

'Yes.'

'Wipe the grin off your face.'

Michael laughed. 'You can't even see me.'

'Yeah, but I know when you're feeling chuffed with yourself.'

'I'm pretty proud of my work, yes. I hope you don't mind me calling so late, but I had to share what I'd discovered.'

'Not at all. I mean I won't sleep again tonight, but it's

worth it.'

'So what should we do? Go and try to see it?'

'I think we should buy it,' Carl stated.

'How? I could probably afford to go over to see it, but that would be my limit. I'm not a full professor yet.'

'That's okay, a patent has come through on one of my designs and my company's stock has jumped in value. I should receive a nice little bonus soon.'

'Little? It'll be more than my salary.'

'A lot more. Which is why I'm happy to pay for both of us to go and bid whatever is necessary for the egg.'

'I know we don't usually talk money, but are you a billionaire?'

Carl chuckled. 'Not yet.'

'I can't allow you to pay for all that.'

'You can and will. You can repay me by popping up to a few distilleries in Scotland afterwards. I've always wanted to do that, particularly with a friend.'

Michael laughed. 'Well, if it helps you achieve a dream.'

'My assistant will make all the arrangements.'

#

The auction house was a large warehouse style building. It was painted dark green and despite renovations, Michael and Carl could sense the history of the place when they walked in. Auctions had been run there for sixty years and they could only ponder the stories behind the artefacts which had been sold there. The auction room was near the front of the building. The auctioneer stood behind a podium on a raised platform, which also displayed each item. Carl and Michael sat near the front. Their item was the eleventh of the day.

'How much are you willing to spend?' Michael asked.

'Whatever it takes.'

'Really? This is all based on a hunch, remember?'

'I know. But this feels right. Your intuition is contagious it seems.'

'As it should be. I'll let you do the bidding since it's your money.'

The auctioneer called out, 'Item 017 in lot 313. Jade egg circa 1900. Can I start the bidding at £25,000?'

The room remained silent. Someone coughed.

'£20,000?' the auctioneer queried. A paddle was raised.

'I have £20,000 at the back of the room. Do I hear £21,000?'

Another paddle went up.

'See if you can work out who we're against,' Carl whispered to Michael. Michael looked around the room as more bids were made.

'The main person is an elderly lady. She looks American.'

'How does someone look American?'

'This is not the time.'

'You're right.'

The bidding had slowed.

'Are you going to bid?'

'£31,000. Going once,' the auctioneer called.

'£32,000,' Carl said as he held up his paddle.

'£34,000,' came the immediate reply from the American lady.

'She's trying to make a knockout bid,' Michael whispered. Carl turned around to look at who he was bidding against. He recognised his competition as someone he'd done business with a decade previously. Even then she was famous for her art related philanthropy.

'She may be willing to bid more than me. That's Eleanor Sprague,' Carl whispered. '£35,000,' he stated confidently.

'£40,000,' came her reply.

'Another knockout bid.'

Carl hesitated.

'Going once. Going twice. For the third and final time. Are we all said and done?' the auctioneer cried out.

'£50,000,' Carl replied. The auctioneer beamed.

'£50,000, going once. Going twice. For the third and final time, are we all done?' He looked expectantly at Eleanor, who shook her head.

'Sold!' He rapped his hammer on the desk.

The next item was a large piece of furniture, which

took some time to move into position. Carl and Michael took the opportunity to move towards the payment and collection point. On their way they passed Eleanor.

'Is that you Carl? Well done.'

'Thank you Eleanor. Good bidding.'

'Not by you. I was done at £40,000,' she said with a smirk. 'See you at the Scipreneur conference next month?'

'Yes. See you then.'

Carl and Michael made their way to the payment counter.

Carl opened his wallet.

'You're paying by credit card?'

'Yes. Cash would be too bulky.' Carl handed his card to the clerk. The clerk confirmed they had the winning paddle number and took the card without hesitation.

'No, I mean you have a high enough credit limit to pay for it?'

'My card is unlimited, Michael.' Carl grinned. 'It's a good thing that bonus I received was a more than I expected. The patent has brought in a lot of money and raised our share price.'

'So now you're worth a few squillion more?'

'Not quite.'

Michael rolled his eyes as the clerk handed them a package. They went outside and sat in the back of their rented car.

Carl opened the box and unpackaged the egg.

'I hope this is worth it,' Michael said.

'Regardless, this has been an adventure and a lot of fun. I say it's been worth every cent even if there is nothing of value here.'

'I agree.'

Carl took out their prize.

'So how do we open it?'

They studied it carefully. The egg was about 15cm long, spinach coloured and made of nephrite. It had silver thread wrapped around it forming a diamond shaped lattice. There were six floral ornaments attached in pairs just below the middle of the egg. Each was made of gold and had a gemstone forming the centre of the flower. There was a barely visible line around the egg's middle.

'I guess we press on the flowers?'

They pressed each of the gemstones in turn. The last one made a clicking sound, but nothing moved.

Carl held the egg in one hand by its base and gently pulled back its top. The egg opened to reveal nothing.

'So after all this, the great egg of truth is empty. Maybe it's trying to say that matter is void, all is vanity?'

'We had no assurances the surprise would still be in there.'

Carl and Michael frowned in disappointment. Michael's frown suddenly grew stronger. 'What's this on the rim?'

They looked closely. There were clear markings where the two halves met. They were spread out and where there were gaps on one side there were markings on the other. Michael took some photos on his phone and zoomed in on the pictures he'd taken.

'It's text,' Michael said excitedly. 'The top edge says, "you … how … I … you … will … true … lies … my … for," and the bottom edge side says, "when … realise … much … value … you … know … love … within … heart … you." When you put them together you get; When you know how much I value you, you will know true love lies within my heart for you.'

Carl smirked. 'Oh, I've longed to hear those words.'

'Oh stop it,' Michael said playfully.

They both slumped.

'I was expecting something more.'

'Me too.'

They stared at the egg, willing it to tell them something more profound.

'Hmph. That's interesting.'

'What?'

'Two of the flowers are a little larger than the others and the way the lattice comes to a point between them makes the shape of a heart.'

Carl pinched the heart and a hidden flap opened to reveal an enamel etching of two teenagers smiling at each other.

'I assume that's Nicholas and his fiancée from their previous meeting?' Michael said.

'Most likely. It was probably meant to be the bride and groom. Well, look at that, the lattice is there not only to make the shape of the heart but to conceal the join and the 'l's on the bottom edge are spaced to conceal the hinge where the flap lifts up.'

'That's probably why the words alternate sides; so the spacing fits.'

'Genius.'

'He really did love her.'

'What do you mean?'

'Don't you see? He thought highly enough of her that he knew she would figure it all out.'

'And when she did, she realised he was worth marrying.'

'Brilliant.'

Carl continued to play with the egg. He removed the enamel etching and turned it around in his hand.

'So is that the universal truth? He loved her?'

'No. The universal truth it would seem is what was written on the back of the enamel picture, which you need to remember was added to or replacing something in the egg by the Prince.'

'Go on then—'

'It says, *No matter where you are in your life, you'll always*

'Perfect,' Michael said.

They sighed contentedly before carefully wrapping up the egg and placing it in its box.

'So where to?'

'The Highlands. Our first distillery and hotel awaits. I think we've earnt the drink we'll get there.'

'Absolutely,' Michael agreed.

# The Second Fear

Raheem looked at the unconscious, blood-covered woman lying on the gurney in front of him and the snarling Doberman being restrained by two men. He knew the dog wasn't rabid, but had been given a cocktail of hormones to make it frighteningly aggressive. Raheem was surprised by the woman's state. Patients normally gave up before their phobia could harm them.

Raheem studied the woman's face and noticed that she, like himself, had a slight bubbling along her eyelids. He picked up her chart and laughed. The people who ran room 101 had made an error. Raheem wheeled the woman's gurney through the treatment centre's labyrinth of hallways to its central station. His supervisor, Sub-Chief Wendy Mendel was sitting behind the island bench like a matriarch marshalling her troops.

'Look at this. They've made a mistake,' he said as he handed over the chart.

'They don't make mistakes.'

'But they've said to transfer her to room 201 when they mean room 102.'

Wendy's face began to contort in a way Raheem had never seen. Was the Sub-Chief … smiling?

'That's not a mistake.'

'But room 102 is where you go to be indoctrinated after room 101.'

'You're so inexperienced.'

'I've been here for seven years.'

'Like I said, you're inexperienced. Room 201 is where we send patients when room 101 fails.'

Raheem frowned. When room 101 failed? Was that even possible?

'I can see you're confused. I'll take it from here.'

Wendy bumped Raheem out of the way and took the gurney. She reached halfway down the corridor before she stopped, sighed and turned towards him.

'I suppose you'd better see this. Come along, hurry up.'

Raheem followed, walking as quickly as he could without breaking into a run.

'Room 101 can fail,' she said as they walked towards an elevator Raheem had seen before, but never been in. 'There are some people who have an inherited condition that destroys the fear producing part of their brain. It doesn't do this until they reach late childhood, so they still have a memory of fear. That's why we don't identify them until after they've been in room 101. Even though we know what their greatest fear was, they're no longer afraid of it. This is where room 201 comes in.'

The elevator doors opened and Raheem followed Wendy and the gurney in. He was surprised there were no buttons. Instead, Wendy placed two fingers against the metal wall and a soft brown light illuminated her fingers. A neutral voice said, 'Identity confirmed. Level two access granted.' The elevator moved downwards.

'Why is room 201 different?'

'After the great failure of a decade ago, we've spent a lot of resources working out what went wrong and why we couldn't break patient UW001.'

Raheem nodded cautiously suddenly remembering the story whispered to him by the person he'd replaced. He'd thought it was a story they'd made up. Now he wasn't so sure.

'So what was the reason?'

'You'll have to wait and see.'

Something about the way Wendy spoke made Raheem think she didn't actually know. When the elevator opened, he tried to take in as much as he could as Wendy charged ahead. Room 201 was twenty metres away, but seemed close given the seemingly endless corridor that stretched on beyond.

The door to room 201 was opened from within as they approached. An elderly man ushered them in. Raheem had never seen anyone who looked so grey. Everything about him, from his clothes to his hair, was a shade of the colour. Even his skin had an unhealthy grey pallor.

'Wendy,' he said in acknowledgement.

'Rupert.'

'Who have you brought me?'

'Patient SM047. The orderly is called Raheem.'

Raheem grimaced. He wasn't an orderly, he was a senior member of the Ministry, almost as senior as Wendy.

'I've waited a long time for this,' Rupert said. He sounded almost gleeful.

'I know. I'm sorry she's still unconscious; they jabbed her while they figured out what to do next. The dog got to her before they realised she wasn't afraid.' Wendy seemed uncharacteristically demure.

'Shame. It's much nicer when they don't bear scars.' Rupert turned to Raheem. 'You understand that fear is essential to our process?'

'Yes, fear is the mind killer that enables us to help the

patient.'

'Not exactly; but we need our specimens to feel it in order for them to switch to the correct way of thinking. It's crucial, not to kill the mind, but to stop people from seeking more than we want them to have; to stop them from wanting what we have.'

Raheem nodded even though he was wondering what would be so wrong about that happening.

Rupert took a breath.

'There are two types of fear. It took patient UW001 to help us understand that. He was an interesting study and the first person we couldn't break in room 101. It turned out he had a very rare condition called Urbach–Wiethe disease. Unfortunately, he died when we tried the next level of treatment. It was a shame, as it seemed like it was working when he passed. I'm grateful you've brought us this patient so we can finally ascertain if we've cracked the secret of fear.'

'What are you going to do?' Raheem asked.

'It's quite straightforward, unlike room 101 where we have to tailor things to the individual. We'll place a breathing mask over her mouth and give her some air to breathe.'

'How will that induce fear?' Raheem asked. He looked across at Wendy and noticed her eyes light up as though he was asking questions she was curious about, but unwilling to ask herself.

Rupert smirked. 'It doesn't. Not until we alter the mix by increasing the carbon dioxide concentration. Our studies with UW001 did not indicate when peak fear could be achieved, but we know it's when the carbon dioxide level is greater than twenty percent.'

'Won't that kill them?'

'No. We keep the oxygen levels high. That's the beauty of it. Their bodies tell them they're suffocating, but the oxygen stops them from suffering any damage. Well, as long as we don't keep the gas on for too long and make their brains tell them to stop breathing. That was the mistake we made last time, but this time we'll get it right.'

'Shall we wake her up?' Wendy asked.

Rupert looked around the room. 'Yes, everything's ready. It's time.'

Rupert handed Wendy a vial and a syringe, and she injected some atropine into the woman's arm. A few moments later patient SM047 stirred.

'Hello, hello,' Rupert said softly.

'Where am I?'

The woman's voice was hoarse.

'You're in room 201. You're strapped to a gurney. It's time to face your fear.'

'I can't.'

'You can.'

'Why are you doing this to me? I keep telling you

people. I haven't felt fear since I was a child.'

Rupert smiled. 'You will now.'

'I don't think so. That dog didn't even scare me. Dogs were my worst fear as a kid.'

'True, and I personally apologise for the failure. We've numbed your wounds so you can focus on what's to come. We think your condition means you cannot feel fear from an external source, but we have reason to believe there is a second type of fear – one that is generated internally when something catastrophic is happening within you. This sensation is usually reserved for people who are dying, but I'm pleased to say, with some certainty, that you will feel fear in a moment.'

Rupert lent in even more closely. 'The way you can stop what we do to you is to wish it upon your son.'

'My son?'

'Yes, you need to wish it upon Nebuchadnezzar.'

She smiled. 'Do your worst to me. It won't happen.'

Rupert placed the mask over her face and turned on the gas. She laughed. 'I told you.'

Rupert said nothing, simply smiled and turned on the carbon dioxide. He observed her closely and spoke to no one in particular. 'It takes a minute or so to see results.'

The woman smiled benignly. Raheem wondered if she thought they were all fools, but her smile waned and turned into a frown and her face contorted into a look of terror. Raheem had seen a lot of people feel fear in his time at the ministry, but something seemed odd about hers. It took him a moment to realise her muscles were twitching while holding the expression.

The woman's eyes bulged, and Raheem could see her mouth open through the mask. Over the years he'd heard a lot of screams, but hers was the most tortured. He thought her cry was accentuated by the novelty of the sensation. Raheem could almost feel every cell in SM047's body sending alarm signals to her brain and forcing her dormant areas to respond— forcing her to feel fear. He shuddered.

Rupert adjusted the gas, and in a few moments her state returned to normal.

'I'm going to do this to you again,' he said. 'That was a mere twenty percent carbon dioxide. This time I'm going to up it to thirty-five.'

Rupert turned the dials with what looked to Raheem like exuberance. The patient immediately began to show signs of panic, thrashing about and trying to free her hands from their bindings to rip the mask off. As the gas started exerting more of an effect, she tried to rub her chin to her shoulder to remove the mask. Raheem could almost see her thinking, 'No!'

She started to cry, and she screamed, 'Do it to Nebby! Just make it stop. Do it to Nebby!'

Rupert beamed. 'We seem to have found the peak

percentage. My superiors will be pleased.'

The patient thrashed even more violently. Raheem was sure her neck would to snap.

'Aren't you going to stop?' Raheem asked.

'Why? We've proven our technique has been perfected.'

'But she did what you asked.'

'Yes, but she won't feel fear again if we let her go. We strongly suspect that if she were freed she would continue her dangerous behaviour.'

'Which was?' Raheem demanded.

'Showing compassion. You see, she's a very trusting and sweet natured individual. We can't have that. What if she breeds and passes on her disease?' Rupert seemed icily serious.

The woman's eyes bulged out of her head before she suddenly went limp, as though unconscious. A few moments later Raheem noticed her pupils dilate, indicating death. Rupert and Wendy watched dispassionately.

'Do you know why we need them to fear us?' Rupert asked.

'I thought so, but I guess not.'

'What we have learnt from her and from UW001 is that an absence of fear leads to the utterly intolerable condition of empathy and compassion. That's why she was brought in.'

'How does one lead to the other?'

'It seems these people, in their absence of fear, have a naturally higher level of empathy and compassion compared to others.' He said the words with such distaste that his expression became a snarl.

'So?'

'You cannot teach empathy, but you can make it flourish by removing fear, so, in order to increase social cohesion all you need to do is to reduce fear— especially fear of other people. This we know can be achieved through things like graduated exposure, shaping, social learning, sustained intergroup contact, super-ordinate goals and so on. This would be disastrous for the social order we've created where a few have all the power and they serve our needs, so we've put in place the means to prevent things changing. In short, we keep people afraid. That's why we're perpetually at war, why there's always an enemy, why there's an us and a them.'

'Why would people being compassionate be a problem?'

'My dear boy, just think! I mean if they worked together, if they worked for each other, they might try to remove us from our positions of power. It would be like the French Revolution all over again, and that would be unacceptable.'

'Couldn't you work with them?'

Rupert looked at Raheem as though he were crazy.

His incredulous expression twisted into a sneer as he pushed a small red button near the door that Raheem hadn't noticed before. When Wendy blinked, Raheem felt like something was wrong. A few moments later two guards came into the room. They looked at Rupert expectantly. He nodded at Raheem.

'What was your name boy?'

'Rah … Raheem.' he stammered. The two guards grabbed an arm each as Raheem realised his fate.

'Take Raheem to room 101,' Rupert said, 'he needs to learn his place.'

# First Constant

It's a Saturday and near the end of my holidays. Sarah and I have been living together for over three months now. She's taken her mother out for lunch in the hills, which are some way from our home, followed by some shopping. The phone rings. Thinking it's Sarah letting me know how her outing was going, I leap up and bound happily towards the phone. It takes me a few moments to comprehend it's John from my work.

'Hi Keith, it's John. I know you're on holidays at the moment but something's happened that you should know about,' John says, his voice catching as he speaks.

My mind's just coming round to 'office' mode when

he says almost absently, 'Stuart's dead.'

In TV shows when someone has bad news to share with someone they say 'you might want to sit down for this'. Now I understand this expression. I even feel my knees give a little and have to reach out for the benchtop to steady myself.

'He was out last night in the country taking photos of lightning and was driving back to the city when he drove head on into a truck. They think he probably fell asleep at the wheel.'

Just a few months ago, Stuart and I had a long conversation about what he wanted to do with his life. He'd decided he wanted to become a meteorologist or a weatherman. He'd even looked at courses he could enrol in. Stuart had always been fascinated by weather, from the simple wonder of how water formed clouds and could create lightning, to the formation of cyclones. He'd tell me how clouds were made of water and they were in fact millions of ice crystals gathered together. He once said with such wonder in his voice that clouds were made from lots of tiny chunks of solid water, which would turn into liquid when they fell from the sky as rain. Of course sometimes rain started as liquid, but he was so amazed at the thought of ice crystals being in clouds and so many other aspects of weather that he wanted to make a career out of it. This was significant since he already had a career, but was prepared to retrain to take on a new one.

'Keith,' he would say to me 'did you know that lightning is one of only two processes that fixate nitrogen from the atmosphere? The other is bacteria.'

One day, probably the third time he'd said this to me, I half-heartedly asked why this was so important. The level of enthusiasm in his response blew me away.

'What do you mean, why is that important? It's vital! It's how life got started. In the beginning there were no nitrogen containing organic molecules. It was lightning strikes in the primordial swamp, soup or whatever you want to call it that created the first nitrogen containing organic compounds – the first amines and nucleotides, the building blocks of proteins and DNA. If it wasn't for lightning we wouldn't be here!'

I had to admit I'd never thought of lightning as being important to life. It's bitterly ironic that it was involved in the end of his.

'He's dead?' I question incredulously. We lapse into silence. Neither of us wants to deal with this unwanted truth.

'How's everyone taking it?' I ask eventually.

'They're pretty shook up. Jenny is especially upset. I'm sitting at my desk, and we're all just quiet. If we look at each other we start crying, so now no one is looking at each other, we just avoid eye contact. No work is being done. We're all in shock. I mean who would have expected this? Stuart was such a crucial member of our team.'

It's true, when Stuart started we began to look forward to him coming in each day as he had a knack for lightening the mood. He single-handedly boosted our department's morale.

John doesn't stop talking. It's as though his grief has suddenly been uncorked and is now flowing out of him. All I want is to get off the phone so I can confront my grief. However, I understand the reason for his emotion. People deal with loss in different ways: Some choose to talk or wail their way through it, some break things, some drink and others prefer to face it head on, internally. I'm the latter type of person. I want to sit in a dark room and work out what this means for me. I want to feel the loss, explore it and most crucially, give it a name. This is not a short process but it's how I deal with grief.

'He had such hope. He was always looking to the future and the possibilities of what could be.' I think I say this, but it could have been John.

Stuart was a daydreamer, like me. He was quirky, very funny and aware. He once turned up to a work function in one of his father's old suits. The suit was brown, worn and the wrong size. It was hilarious and a definite conversation starter. When asked why he'd worn it, Stuart responded with a twinkle in his eye and a genial shrug of his shoulders.

'The funeral is on Tuesday at the Necropolis. It's at one. Can you make it?' John asks.

'Sure.' I'll have to cancel a round of golf I had planned with my brother.

'Great,' John says as though my presence will somehow make him feel better.

'Everyone from work is going to wear their blue shirts.'

Last Christmas our boss got everyone the same polo shirt with our company logo on it. Stuart was the only one who wore his. Wearing it to the funeral seems like a fitting tribute.

'Okay, I'll wear mine too.'

We pause briefly; I hope that like me, picturing Stuart in his blue shirt is bringing a bittersweet smile to John's face.

'There will be a reception at his parent's place afterwards. Can you come to that too?'

'Sure,' I say again. I've only been there once before. Stuart's parents must be devastated. I can't imagine what it must be like to lose a child; nevertheless a fresh wave of grief washes over me as I empathise with them.

'I'll see you there,' John says before he hangs up. It's clear we were both in the process of bursting into tears.

\#

A short while later Sarah breezes in. She's full of energy, excitement and shopping bags, and she doesn't notice

I'm upset.

'You'll never guess what I found out today,' she says excitedly.

I open my mouth to speak but no words come out. Even if they had I don't think they would have stopped her continuing.

'Mum and Dad are planning to sell our home. I mean their home!'

I nod, simply to acknowledge her statement. Sarah finally notices I'm upset. In a way that I don't fully appreciate until much later, her problem is instantly forgotten.

'What's wrong?' she asks softly.

'I had a call while you were out—'

I realise how shattered I'm feeling and tears well in my eyes. Sarah reaches out and hugs me.

'My friend Stuart was killed in a car crash.'

Saying it aloud makes it seem more real and a fresh wave of grief washes over me. I realise I'm crying. This is the first time Sarah has seen me cry, but I'm unashamed.

She holds me tightly and softly rubs my back. I allow Sarah inside my vulnerability and give over to my emotion. If I wasn't in love with her before this moment, I am now.

We stand like this for a few minutes before we sit on the couch and face each other.

'How'd it happen?' she asks quietly.

I tell her about the accident and what he was doing out late at night in a storm. I realise if he was asleep at the wheel he probably died instantly and dreaming about what he loved.

'There's a funeral on Tuesday. We're all going to wear those tacky work shirts as a tribute to him.'

'Did you want me to come? I can try to get out of my business trip.'

I enjoy the occasional days we get apart from each other when she takes her business trips. I feel they make us stronger as a couple. It's said that absence makes the heart grow fonder, but I prefer to think of it as giving me a chance to miss her so I can appreciate her presence.

'No, that's okay. Go on your trip. I'll be all right.' I quietly appreciate the opportunity to grieve my way.

We spend much of the next hour speaking in fragments. The odd question is asked and answered. The odd comment is made and acknowledged. Slowly, the shock subsides. Eventually we prepare some food. I don't even notice what it is. We go to bed where a restless, disturbed sleep awaits me. In the morning I help Sarah pack and a taxi takes her to the airport. She gives me a gentle kiss and a long lingering hug as she says goodbye.

#

It's the day of the funeral. The last two days have felt as

though they occurred in slow motion. Several times I have found myself thinking about things I'd like to discuss with Stuart and then tear up as I realise this will not be possible. I arrive at the cemetery well before the service and meet up with the rest of the people from work. We greet each other in monotones. Our matching shirts act as a bond between us. Our shared sense of mourning brings us together. We slowly shuffle into the hall for the eulogies.

They play a piece of music that was one of Stuart's favourites. It is *O' Fortuna* from the *Carmina Burana*. The line '*Ludo mentis aciem*' sums up Stuart admirably. It very loosely translates to 'deceptive sharp mind.' The intensity of the song produces a physiological response. It is uplifting and tragic all at once. I think of the song I would like played at my funeral – '*Soulfly*' *(Eternal Spirit Mix)* by Soulfly. Stuart would have liked that piece of music too.

As the song plays, I have time to notice how upset everyone is. Their sadness is a measure of what he brought to our lives. Knowing Stuart enriched us and losing him has devastated our world. I look at the coffin and know that I'm crying. As I reflect on Stuart's impact on my life the thought that it could be Sarah in the coffin occurs to me. This is when I really lose control and break down completely. When I lost my parents I wasn't this inconsolable.

The music ends. An invitation for the next speaker is made.

Jenny from work gets up to speak. She tells two stories about Stuart.

'I remember one day Stuart came into the office in a bad mood. He was running late and had sped to work in his new car. We all knew Stuart's beat up old car had recently died and his new car was his pride and joy. He got caught speeding and was issued with a fine, which made him even later. Then, because he was rushing when he parked the car he reversed a little too quickly and ran the back of it into a tree. The resulting dent was only small, but to Stuart it might as well have been a dent on his life. He was fuming as he got out of the car. A stranger got out of a car near him and walked over. They asked what was wrong. Stuart's response was that he was late for work, had just got a speeding fine and had just crashed his car. Then he added that to top it all off there was a new manager starting today who was meant to be a real arsehole. The person he was talking to then responded with 'I'm the new manager.' Stuart's response was to say 'oh fuck' and storm off to our office. He acted out the story for us complete with all the emotion. It was one of the funniest things I've ever heard.'

I remember that story well. It really was hilarious. We'd teased Stuart mercilessly about it for weeks. Perhaps not surprisingly he and the new manager didn't get along well after that. I look around to see if she's here and am shocked that she isn't. Eventually, I spot her coming in late and sitting in the back row. At least she's wearing her blue shirt.

'Another time when I'd been working in the office for a few months, Keith said something sarcastic to me…'

What me sarcastic? Never. Then I realise that's exactly what Stuart would have said.

'… and in response, I gave him the finger. He laughed and said "touché". Stuart saw the whole thing and within a minute had created and printed off a certificate for me. The certificate basically said welcome to the team. Now that I'd felt confident enough to give someone the finger, I was accepted. The certificate was labeled as being for outstanding achievement. Stuart later had it laminated for me and made me keep it on my desk.'

The fact that I knew the two stories makes me feel closer to Stuart and as though I knew him well. Jenny has done a remarkable job with her speech. Her voice has maintained its strength and she's hardly faltered. But now, as she comes to concluding her speech her voice starts to crack, bringing a lump to my throat.

'Stuart was a remarkable man. Witty, quirky and kind. When we first met, he asked me out many times and I said no. That was because at the time I didn't really know him. After the fifth time I told him to stop asking me out. He never asked me out again.'

This is when the tears start flowing on her face. Her voice breaks as she attempts to choke back the tears.

'I wish he had, but he was a man of his word. Stuart I will miss you.'

The last words are said with a rush as she completely breaks down. She's led from the podium by John who provides her with tissues and support. If he hadn't helped her I don't think she'd have been able to return to her seat.

Other speakers get up and eulogise Stuart. His parents speak. They're clearly devastated. No parent should outlive their child and Stuart's are no exception. They barely manage to get their words out, yet the power and strength of their emotion is overwhelming. There are no dry eyes here. When they finish everyone is asked to walk past the coffin. We've been given flowers to place around it.

One by one.

One by one we file past the closed coffin.

One by one we say our goodbyes.

One by one we place our white roses around him.

Our loss unites us. Our grief overwhelms us.

He was our friend, our colleague.

He was *my* friend, *my* colleague.

Forever more, when lightning strikes I'll think of

him.

The wannabe weatherman, the comedian and the professional.

He will be mourned.

Stuart is so still inside his coffin. For someone who was so full of energy and life this seems out of place. His stillness captivates me. This must be the most still he's ever been. Yet, I remind myself that he's not still. The earth is spinning; therefore he's moving relative to space, although not relative to me in the room. If you were on the equator and sat down, you wouldn't be still, you'd be moving at over a thousand miles an hour. The logic for this is simple. The earth's circumference at the equator is roughly forty thousand kilometres, and the earth rotates once in twenty-four hours. Therefore, even sitting in the same spot for a whole day you would have moved forty thousand kilometres through space. Divide this by twenty-four hours and you get 1,666 kilometres per hour as your speed. The most still you can be is at the North or South Pole. There the rotation of your limbs would trace out a circle of about one and a half metres in circumference, thus you would only be moving at about 0.00006 kilometres per hour, which is not quite, not moving, but is the best you can manage on Earth.

I imagine telling Stuart all this. He would have loved the idea and the implications for the concepts of being peaceful and restful. He would have also loved linking the concept of stillness to invisibility and we would have discussed how ninjas claim to be able to become invisible yet what they really mean is to be so still that the human eye isn't able to detect them because they make no movement for the eye to catch. A suitably camouflaged ninja would therefore not be seen and be invisible. We'd both be amused at the thought that the most invisible you could be would be at either pole, even though we would acknowledge the flaw in the logic that led to that conclusion. We'd laugh at the image of a white suited ninja sitting down surrounded by snow and ice and at what we'd say to such a person.

Stuart would have been open to talking about the nature of what it means to be at rest and at peace. The meaning of these words has never been more apparent to me than now. I'm definitely not at peace. I ache internally and existentially. I've lost my friend and a fellow armchair philosopher. He is the one at rest; his time on this earth is over. I try to tell myself that he's become part of the cosmic holograph and part of the sum of histories of the world and that this is also the fate that awaits me. As ideas they're fine to discuss, but they do nothing to comfort me now.

#

We've made our way to Stuart's parents' home. It's a small red brick home with high ceilings and a lot of character. No one has said much since leaving the funeral. I pass on my condolences to Stuart's parents who are trying to remain stoic, but still have to leave the room every few minutes to regain some control over their emotions. His parents comment to me that the house felt empty when Stuart moved out, but now it seems even more empty somehow. Their only child has died and I'm unsure of what to say to them. I tell them how much I enjoyed talking to Stuart and how he could always bring a smile to my face no matter what mood I was in. I tell them he was a fine individual who was extremely professional and brilliant at his job. I tell them I'll miss him and his company immensely. They smile politely and thank me for my kind words. They will hear similar sentiments from some fifty odd people this afternoon. I don't know if that will help or simply remind them of how much they've lost. Nevertheless, I know that people will want to tell them their stories of Stuart and that his parents will listen respectfully and thank each person because that is a measure of who they are.

I move over to my colleagues. They're discussing the accident. Everyone is speaking slowly and in hushed tones. There are pauses between each person's statement and the next response.

'What about the truck driver? The poor guy must be crushed,' John says. Despite the solemnity of the situation my brain flits out the thought, but not as crushed as Stuart. I keep this to myself.

'Apparently, he's very upset. Remember he was just someone doing their job when all of a sudden he's become involved in killing someone else,' John says.

'That must have been horrific,' Jenny agrees quietly.

'Especially since it wasn't really his fault. The police and everyone have cleared him of doing anything wrong,' Joe, the final member of our office team, says.

I can only imagine what it must be like to be responsible for ending someone's life. I feel pity for the truck driver, it must be a heavy burden to bear.

'Makes you think though doesn't it?' Joe questions. 'I mean if Stuart can be taken from us so suddenly…' He trails off.

I accepted my mortality a long time ago and am comfortable with the concept of dying. John, Jenny and Joe (who Stuart used to call 'Triple J' behind their backs) appear to have yet to conquer their fear of death. I stop myself from saying that death is part of life and part of the natural order of things. This would sound flippant and uncaring at this point in time. Instead, I empathise with them.

'Yeah I know, it's tough. Any of us could go at any time. And Stuart was still so young.'

'Remember when he came to Joe's fancy dress party as Cupid?' John asks.

'Yeah it was hilarious— It takes a lot of guts to dress

up in a giant nappy and go to a party,' I say. 'I mean think about it. After the initial humour wears off you have to spend the rest of the evening in a nappy.'

'Yeah, but Stuart pulled it off,' John says with a half-smile.

'If anyone could it was him,' Joe says.

'He kept shooting Jenny with his bow and arrow,' I say. John, Joe and I laugh. Jenny looks sad. John and Joe don't notice and continue.

'Yeah he wouldn't stop all night,' Joe says.

'Yeah Jenny why wouldn't you give him a kiss?' John says, chiming in like we're back in the office.

Jenny blushes. 'He wouldn't leave me alone and I didn't want to encourage him— I do regret it now though.'

That's what we all seem to be feeling now: regret. Regret that we hadn't socialised more with Stuart and hadn't given enough appreciation to what he brought to our team.

We continue trading stories of Stuart for a while. It's clear that he has touched our lives in a positive way. Slowly people start to leave making a final expression of sorrow to Stuart's parents as they exit.

#

Sarah returns home the next day. She spends a lot of time simply sitting near me, letting her presence be her support. She understands that words are not what I need now. They'll come eventually, but for the moment this is what I want. As I mourn, I acknowledge part of me is declaring its love for Sarah. I wouldn't have expected her to understand my needs so well, so completely. I realise that not only am I in love with her, but that she is with me.

# Sever-Reign

The Queen had finished her breakfast and was turning her attention to her fresh pot of tea, when her butler, James, knocked on her sitting room door.

'Ma'am, the Prime Minister is here to see you.'

'Really? She wasn't on my appointment list.'

'No, Ma'am. She says this is a private matter and she doesn't want it recorded.'

'How intriguing. Show her in.'

'Yes Ma'am.'

The Queen watched as the elegant, grey haired lady entered the room. The Prime Minister looked like a shell of the person who'd won an election a year ago. She

carried a folder that was marked TOP SECRET –
HM/PM EYES ONLY.

'Your Majesty, I—'

'Eleanor, you look exhausted, let me get you some
tea.'

'You're too kind.'

The Queen rang a small bell. The Queen knew the
tinkle was only a conceit for her benefit, as the bell had
a motion sensor that triggered an alert outside the room.
In a moment, James reappeared.

'Ma'am?'

'A cup for Eleanor, please. I'll pour it from my pot.'

'Yes, Ma'am.'

James soon returned with a china cup and saucer. He
placed it in front of the PM and quickly disappeared
again.

'So, Eleanor, what brings you here so early this
morning?'

'Your Majesty, I apologise for coming unannounced
and at such an hour, but some information about the
U.S. President came to light last night that couldn't wait.'

'I thought this was a private matter?'

'It is… I'm not sure how to say it though.'

'I can only act on what I know, so tell me.'

'Let me put it this way. If you could go back in time
and kill Hitler, would you?'

'Oh, I say. What a question…' The Queen gave the

idea some thought, 'No, I wouldn't.'

'Why not?'

'Killing Hitler would be unlikely to stop the war. He may have been the figurehead we know, but someone worse could have risen to that position if he wasn't there. I mean what if they'd been a better strategist? They might have won. So no, I would not kill Hitler. Mengele on the other hand… those poor children.' The Queen shook her head in disgust.

The Queen watched as Eleanor pondered her response. The reply must not have been what she was expecting.

'What if you could be certain there was about to be a war and you could stop it from eventuating?'

'Now that is a different question. Would anyone say no to preventing a war?'

'They shouldn't.'

'Why don't you tell me what this is really about? You didn't come here to discuss philosophy.'

'No, Your Majesty, I didn't. I apologise for not getting to the point. Some information has come to hand that needs to be dealt with. Something I'd like you to consider taking a leading role in—'

'Eleanor, you know I cannot lead you into battle.'

'Yes, Your Majesty. I think though when you see what's in this folder, you might consider the unorthodox course of action I have in mind.'

Eleanor passed the folder to the Queen, who carefully untied the string that was wound in a figure eight to seal the binder. The binder opened to reveal a screen on the left and a sheaf of paper on the right.

'So what is in here?'

'I think it speaks for itself.' Eleanor took out her phone and started replying to emails, while the Queen read through the document.

'Hmm.'

'But that would mean—'

'Yes, Your Majesty.'

'—Their election was rigged?'

'Not only theirs. Keep reading.'

The Queen kept reading, giving the occasional gasp. Meanwhile, Eleanor tapped away on her phone.

'Is he really a genius and not a buffoon?'

'Apparently so. Watch the video.'

The Queen clicked on the screen. 'I don't believe it.'

A few minutes later, the Queen asked, 'And you're certain of the veracity of this information?'

'I wouldn't be here if there were any doubt. We were lucky that the person who found it handed it to one of our double agents and that they both accepted asylum with us. Keep reading.'

Ten minutes later the Queen felt her face going cold as the blood drained from her skin. She realised she was going into shock.

'So if I read this correctly, every major election since 2015 has been compromised? — What about France?'

'The way the program works is by boosting the underdog's vote in key areas, but they need to be polling over thirty percent for it to work. In France, the final round was between two candidates. The algorithm couldn't do its thing. Plus their President took two-thirds of the vote, which was too high for the algorithm to deny.'

'I see. That I accept. What I cannot accept is that all this was masterminded by that man. He's giving the orders, even to Russia?'

'I found it hard to believe too. But as you can see, the information was checked more than once. It's all to do with the training. You can do a lot if you're properly trained.'

'What are you going to do about this?'

'That's why I'm here—' Eleanor paused, as though she were unsure how to continue. 'As you can see, other than the two operatives and myself no one else knows about this. If he dies this process stops. No one else can activate or decode the tech used and no one else even knows about it. What I'd like, Your Majesty, is for you to kill him.'

'You want me to kill the American President?'

'Yes.'

'No.'

'Yes, Your Majesty. The message it would send, coming from you, would restore people's faith in leadership, right at the time it's being questioned.'

'Why not release the information? Let the people go after him themselves.'

'There are two reasons. First, were this information to become known it would destroy democracy. Full stop. No one would trust governments, elections or the fundamental aspects of democracy. There would be violence, civil war, and even world war.'

'Yes, I see. And the second?'

'Do you remember Coventry and the blitz? We chose not to act on the intelligence we'd received from cracking Enigma, as it would alert the enemy that we knew how to read their messages. It cost us five hundred and sixty-eight lives, plus thousands in injuries. However, it gave us a strategic advantage that wound up saving many times more.'

'That was the decision of the Prime Minister. Not the monarch.'

'You're right, Your Majesty. But you have a unique ability to get close to him and achieve the outcome while restoring pride in our system and keeping diplomatic relations open between our countries. If we went with a sniper or someone anonymous, it could be spun by his supporters that the people they perceive as enemies were responsible, or worse a terrorist group could claim responsibility and confirm the biased beliefs of his supporters. It needs to be public so the message can be controlled.'

They sat in an uncomfortable silence. Both took sips of their lukewarm tea without comment. The Queen sighed. 'The lessons from the peace process are clear; whatever life throws at us, our individual responses will be all the stronger for working together and sharing the load. I do not give you laws but I can do something else —I can give my devotion to the peoples of our brotherhood of nations. For this reason, I'll do what you ask.'

'Thank you, You Majesty.' Eleanor began packing up the files.

'On your way out ask James to send for a copy of Arthur Conan Doyle's biography for me.'

'Your Majesty?'

'Eleanor?'

'Sorry, Your Majesty. Right away,' she replied as she walked briskly to the door. Ten minutes later James knocked, entered the room and handed the Queen the book she was after.

#

Two weeks later, the President and the Queen were about to meet at the Palace. The Queen knew the President would accept an invite to a private meeting with royalty, particularly as she put a phrase on the invite about wanting to talk to a man of his stature.

She checked that everything was ready. Two pots of tea were steeping, and a plate of petits fours sat waiting to be consumed. A moment later there was a knock on the door and James introduced the American President. A security agent entered with him. The Queen asked for the guard to wait outside. A nod from the President and at last they were alone. The Queen motioned for the President to sit down, thereby avoiding shaking hands, since she knew the President did not like the action.

'Mr. President,' she began.

'Beatrice.'

'It's Your Majesty, Mr President.'

'Oh sorry.'

'Please sit down and let me pour you some tea.' The President sat in a gilded chair, looking smug, while the Queen poured them each a cup of tea from their respective pots. The Queen took a sip of hers and confirmed it was the right temperature.

'The Yellow Jasmine tea I have prepared for you is very special. It was used by the creator of Sherlock Holmes as a tonic to promote his health and vitality. I remembered reading about it in his biography, so I looked it up for your visit. It's made from a plant called Gelsemium, which we have in our garden. Very pretty flowers. I believe he liked to drink it in one go as he convinced himself it was more effective that way.'

The Queen wondered if the President would take the bait. He did, and drank it in a few gulps. The trouble with playing a role, is that you have to behave in accordance with it.

'Arthur Conan Doyle started off with very small doses of the tea and slowly worked his way up. He got up to twelve millilitres and then stopped as he felt the side effects were too severe. I've given you twenty-four millilitres, just to be safe.'

'Huh?' the President grunted.

'The tea. It's poisonous.' The Queen watched the President scrunch his face in confusion.

'You should probably tell your serviceman to enact the protocol for the death of yourself. I don't know what yours is called. Mine is Operation London Bridge. We know about '*assumo*' and what you've done with it.'

'How can you know about that?'

'The person who created it for you went to your government. Fortunately, the agent they went to also worked for us.' The President's face was starting to redden. The Queen knew it was due to the relaxation of his blood vessels and that a mild paralysis would be setting in. The President struggled to stand. He staggered towards the door, while the Queen sat and took another sip of tea. She watched him fumble with the handle and almost fall out of the room. A moment later both of their security personnel rushed into the room. The Queen's agent stood next to her.

The American agent yelled, 'Why aren't you arresting her?'

The Queen's agent said, 'She… she has immunity.'

'She murdered him.'

'Yes, but she's the Queen. She can't be charged with any crime.'

The Queen realised that was probably why Eleanor had asked her.

#

A few minutes later, the Queen spoke to an assembly of reporters, explaining why she'd taken the course of action she had, in accordance with the story she'd agreed with Eleanor. She reached the end of her speech as it had been written, took a breath and added words that would surprise the Prime Minister. 'Today I've chosen to act in accordance with my heart, despite the cost of a life. However, my actions should be seen for what they were. I hereby implore the parliament to pass an act enabling me to abdicate. At such time, I will leave the grounds of this palace so that I may be arrested. I ask for no special treatment and wish to face justice for my crime. What leadership would I be showing if I did less?'

The applause reinforced her decision.

# The Principled Principal

Peter heard some students shouting at each other. He paused, wondering if he should intervene now, or let the situation escalate to give him something he might be able to use to his advantage. A few moments later a scuffle broke out and Peter knew he had the perfect test for the new principal. He walked over, separated the students and corralled them towards the administration building.

'Sir, um, I'm bleeding,' Cecily said meekly. A thin line of blood was visible on her arm.

'Fine, off you go to the sick bay. I could see you weren't at fault anyway.'

'Thanks Mr Saul.' Cecily seemed relieved to get away

as she veered away from the group.

They soon reached the administration building and Peter saw the principal sipping coffee and talking to his assistant, James. Greg interacted easily with James which annoyed Peter as James didn't get on well with him.

'Greg, I have some students for you,' Peter said with a slight edge to his voice. He didn't like the new principal and wasn't afraid to show it. It wasn't because Greg was black; there was just something about his confidence and charm that made Peter distrustful. Plus, Peter had thought he was going to be given the job, especially after making it to the last round of interviews and all his years at the school.

'Okay. You two go wait in my office,' Greg said. 'I'll just have a quick word with Mr Saul.'

The students dutifully slunk down the short hallway and into the principal's office. From the foyer Peter could see them take a seat. They both crossed their arms and looked away from each other. The hostility coming from Gwen was palpable even from this distance.

'What have they done?' Greg asked.

'It seems Gwen, Cecily and Jack got into a bit of a fight in the cafeteria.'

'Over what?'

'We'll, it seems Jack had talked Cecily into buying him lunch. Unfortunately, he was quite showy about it, and Gwen took offence and it started a fight between the three of them. That's why Cecily isn't here. She's in the sick bay getting a minor abrasion tended to. She was just trying to be nice.'

#

Greg paused for a moment. He knew Peter didn't like him and was probably using this situation to test him. He decided to teach Peter a lesson on the difference between leadership and management.

'I'll make you a deal, Peter. Give me five minutes. If they don't come out smiling and at peace with each other you won't have to come and have a coffee with me each Friday recess for the rest of the semester.'

Peter was clearly surprised by Greg's response and the strange terms of the deal.

Peter shrugged his shoulders in concession. 'Fine,' he said through gritted teeth, before giving a half-smile. Greg could tell Peter thought there was no way he'd be able to deliver his side of the bargain.

As Greg walked into his office, he tapped an image of a chess clock which he'd taped above his door on his first day. 'Five minutes. You can start timing now.'

Greg watched Peter look at his watch, then sit on a chair in the foyer to wait.

'Greetings, students,' Greg said amiably.

Despite their mood, Greg watched Gwen and Jack look at each other. They were clearly bemused by his turn of phrase. Greg paused and gave them a long look, reading their body language and facial expressions while developing the course of action he'd been considering. The momentary silence did nothing to ease the tension that hung in the air.

'I'm going to do you two a favour,' Greg announced abruptly, once again surprising the students. 'Jack, do you like Gwen?'

'Huh?'

'Do you like her as a friend?'

'Yes,' Jack admitted sheepishly.

'And Gwen, do you like Jack as a friend?'

'Yes,' she replied quietly.

'Good. Now the thing that strikes me is that we have two people who like each other, yet are clearly also upset with each other, because what, one of you was friendly with someone else? This leads me to the conclusion that you in fact like each other more than you've stated to one another. It strikes me that you probably know or suspect the other person likes you as more than friends, otherwise you, Jack, would not have attempted to play Cecily against Gwen, and you Gwen would not have been jealous or as annoyed with Cecily or Jack if you didn't like him as more than a friend. Let's get this out in the open. Jack, do you like Gwen as more than a friend? Gwen, do you like Jack as more than a friend?'

They both hesitated.

'Come now, this is no time to be bashful.'

'Yes,' they mumbled in unison, before turning and smiling shyly at each other.

'Good, now let me give your relationship a kickstart. Jack stop being a fool and show some strength of character. If you start a relationship with less than one hundred percent commitment, it's doomed to failure, and this is true for any endeavour. Gwen, don't assume that Jack knows how you feel, just tell him. Any relationship without clear communication is also doomed to fail.'

Greg dramatically intoned each "doomed to fail".

'Now comes the real favour, I suggest that you become boyfriend and girlfriend. How many classes do you have together?'

'Three,' Gwen said. She and Jack looked like they'd just entered an alternate universe.

'Excellent. You should sit next to each other in class. Let your proximity to each other be the sign that you're a couple. Learn to bask in the presence of the other person and let that be your display of your affection as this is the secret for true intimacy – But no making out on campus … okay? It upsets other students. You may however, hold hands.'

'Okay,' they said in unison. It was clear to them they had no choice but to agree. Greg wondered if they realised the no kissing was because of his own views, rather than other students, but it was worth a shot. He cast a quick glance at the clock in his office. There wasn't long left.

'Good. Now as it stands, Gwen, I have to call your parents and give you a detention for fighting with another student. You've broken the rules and I have to be seen to be enforcing consequences. Here's what I propose: that I also do the same for Jack. Let's say he swore at me or something. The two of you can then report to me on Friday after school for an hour. Call it an unconventional first date. Agreed?'

They nodded, too stunned to respond.

'Good, now the two of you need to go to class. You both also need to apologise to Cecily, yes?'

They nodded again.

'Okay, now off you go.'

They left, each with a stupefied smile on their faces. Greg looked at the clock. By his estimate, he had fifteen seconds to go.

Greg leant against the doorframe and made eye contact with Peter. He watched him meet the students as they walked out. It was clear that Peter was disturbed to see they were smiling. Greg could just hear Peter as he stopped the students. 'Let me guess, he didn't punish you?'

'No he did. We both have afterschool detentions,' Jack replied.

'And our parents are being called,' Gwen added.

'Then, did he ask you to come out smiling?'

'No,' Gwen said, clearly puzzled by the question.

'Then why are you smiling?' Peter asked.

Neither student could find the words to explain what had happened, so they shrugged their shoulders. As they continued past Peter, they took each other's hands. Peter continued to watch them. Even when viewing them from behind, it was clear they were still grinning from ear to ear.

#

*Twenty years later*

One Saturday morning, Peter went to his favourite café for a late breakfast and some quiet time. He sat in his usual seat and looked up to the register. He got the nod he expected from the barista who he knew would soon bring him his regular order of eggs on toast and a coffee. He noticed that a man paying for their meal looked familiar, but then so did a decent portion of the people he met – an occupational hazard of being a teacher for thirty-five years. The man finished paying, and as they headed for the door they made eye contact.

'Aren't you Mr Saul?' The 'mister' definitely meant it was a former student.

'Yes, I'm sorry but you'll have to remind me of who you are.' As the words left his mouth it hit him.

'Wait, it's you! James, no wait, Jack.'

'What do you mean "it's me?"'

Peter had to stop himself from giving Jack a hug. Instead, he simply held out his hand and as they shook he said, 'Thank you.'

'What for?' Peter could see Jack was confused. He hadn't had a lot to do with Mr Saul when he was at school, and now he was being thanked for something. Peter motioned for him to take the seat opposite, and Jack obediently sat in the chair.

'For making me lose a bet.'

'Huh?'

'When you and Gwen got into trouble that day, I made a bet with Mr Solomon that he couldn't get you to be at peace with each other within five minutes. I lost, and as a result had to meet with him every week for the rest of the semester for coffee.'

'That doesn't sound like you lost, or did you have to pay for the coffee?'

Peter laughed. 'No, when Mr Solomon became principal, I wanted the job too, but he got it over me and I was pissed. He saw my hostility and knew I wouldn't work with him, so he found a way for me to get to know him and to see why he was the right choice to lead the school.'

Peter paused. He couldn't help but stop and think about the ingenious strategy that had been used against him. 'I always thought he kept me close in a 'keep your friends close but your enemies closer' way, and I even accused him of that in one of our Friday morning coffees. He laughed and said that wasn't it and when I figured out what he was actually trying to teach me, I'd be ready to lead my own school.'

'So what was it?'

'It took a few years and then one day I was teaching a class George Orwell's *1984*. We were discussing its conclusion and what we could learn from it when … I think it might have been Gwen's sister … said it teaches us that the greatest victory is not in the mind or over the self, but when you can turn an enemy into a friend. I realised this was how I'd presented to Mr Solomon when he started. Yet here we were just a couple of years later and he'd become a great friend. I mean we were really close; our families would go away together and we'd have dinner at each other's houses. Anyway, I was thinking about all this and it hit me that he'd turned me, his enemy, into his friend. The thing is that despite how close we'd become I still thought of him as someone who was just trying to find a way to work with me, but after that my understanding of our relationship changed and I treated him differently.'

'Yeah, he kind of had an impact upon people.'

'Anyway it only took him a week or so to notice. He marked the occasion by bringing his bottle of Galileo whisky to school and calling me into his office after school one Friday. He ritualistically poured the Scotch into his special tulip shaped glasses, and proposed a toast. Naturally, I asked him to what? He replied to whatever deus ex machina made me finally realise what he'd been trying to teach me. Not for the first time I was mute with awe. How he'd divined my epiphany I don't know, but he had. After that, he kept trying to get me to apply for principal positions in other schools, but I still felt I had more to learn from him, so I stayed. When he retired last year I took over as principal of our school.'

'Something's been bugging me for years. Was it my imagination or was there actually a chess clock above his office door?' Jack asked, abruptly changing the conversation.

'It's gone now. But yes, after I lost our bet I replaced the picture of one with a real one. He became famous amongst staff for his five minute meetings. His philosophy was that if a problem couldn't be solved in that amount of time then it required input from other sources or more considered thought to make the decision. He believed such thought should occur independently so that no one person's perspective unduly influenced the information that was feeding into the decision. Either way the meeting should end as the issue was not going to be resolved at that point in time. Now the clock's been replaced by a sign that says ex-office of the deus ex machina.'

'Huh?'

'In literature, when a novel is ambling along and needs to be concluded and there's some form of unexpected or left field solution that suddenly presents itself it's known as the god of the machine, or deus ex machina. To me Mr Solomon was conceptually similar to that for what he did for our school. You may not have noticed in your time, but our student numbers and results were falling and staff were desperately trying to leave, but Mr Solomon turned all that around in the nick of time. I later found out that had the trend continued for another year or two we would have been shut down or merged with another school. Anyway, to me he was always the deus ex machina for our school. I liked that it could also mean he was the master of the school 'machine'. When I told him it had become my personal nickname for him, he laughed and said, but don't you get that I'm trying to lead for when I'm not there? You are all the deuces of the machine. It's what you do by being a teacher. You are the intervention that brings about success.'

'Wow, what an attitude to have towards staff! I wish my boss was like that.'

'Yes, he was a one of kind. Did you know that there's a celebration for him at the school on Friday at 4.00pm?'

'No. What for?'

'Oh, I thought you'd have heard. He passed away last week.'

'Shit no. I'm sorry.'

'If he meant that much to you, you should come.'

'I will. I'd like to express my gratitude.'

'Maybe you could write him a letter? Not a typed one, an old-fashioned handwritten one. He'd like that, and I think a few people are planning on doing it.'

The barista walked over carrying a plate in one hand and a coffee in the other. He placed them on the table. Jack took the opportunity to stand.

'Yeah, okay. Thanks for letting me know. I'll leave you to have your breakfast in peace.'

Jack pushed in his chair.

'It was great to run into you,' Peter said. 'Do you still talk to Gwen? If so say hi from me.'

Jack nodded. 'I will.'

Peter watch him leave. A tear welled in his eye as he contemplated how many lives Greg had affected.

#

Jack arrived at the celebration a little after 4pm. The school's gymnasium was filled with people. Most were talking in small groups in hushed tones. Jack wondered if he'd run into any of his old classmates. He took out the letter he'd written and read through it one last time.

*Dear Mr Solomon,*

*How to express my gratitude? It seems silly, but many years ago and in just five minutes you changed my life. I ran into Mr Saul the other day and it turns out that mine was not the only life altered that day. The thought that really gets me is that you probably don't even remember us! I mean we were five minutes of your life twenty years ago. I like to think you do remember Gwen and me and that we had at least some impact upon you, given the impact you had on us. I mean the things you told us that day. Now that I'm older and have had a chance to put your lessons into practice, they changed my life. When you told Gwen and I to bask in the presence of the other person, you did not make sense to us, particularly as hormonal teenagers. But then a day or two later we were in class and our knees touched and we both smiled and somehow just felt peace. It was like the touch discharged our pent up energy. In that space of contentment, which became a feature of our classes together, we could focus on the subject being taught to us. Did you know that after our meeting with you our grades went up for the classes we had together? What really surprised me was that even though we took your advice and did not make out (much) at school, everyone still knew we were a couple and in fact we became the couple everyone wanted to be like. It was as though our relationship was more real than everyone else's. Gwen and I also spoke at length about what you meant by starting things with a commitment to following them through. This really changed how we approached our studies, our relationship and later, our jobs. You may be surprised to know that Gwen and I did break up after being together for six years, but this was not due to our relationship falling apart, if that makes any sense. Perhaps, because we (once again in accordance with your advice) communicated well, we realised our vocations were pulling us in different directions, geographically speaking, and that we couldn't both have success and remain a couple. So we changed the status of our relationship and declared ourselves unboyfriend and ungirlfriend, much the same way you did the reverse for us. We're still great friends and talk fortnightly, but each of us are in other relationships now. It's funny though, when each of us met our new partners we entered our relationships with 100% commitment and you know what? We found ourselves explaining the suggestions you made to us to them and it really made a difference. It's like it fast forwarded the relationship and not having to go through the month or so of uncertainty about its status, which then implants the association of doubt with that person, we just started strong and remained that way. It also took Gwen and I time to understand why you wanted us to tone down the physical side of our relationship – it meant delaying umm ... consummating ... it and that meant by the time we did it was an expression of our love rather than our lust. Even though it may not have been your intent, you taught us so much about relationships and how to lead our lives. I mean we both have had success in our jobs, because we were employed by organisations we could commit to 100%. Mr Saul said*

Jack wiped a tear from his eye, folded the letter and put it in its envelope. He walked over to where a memorial had been set up and placed it in a box that was shaped like an old-fashioned metal postbox. He was the seventeenth person to make the gesture that day. He was not the last.

## La Criminal

The woman wearing blue scrubs was sympathetic. 'We give her something that puts her to sleep and something that stops the heart.'

It was a sunny autumn morning and my German Shepard, Brandy was whimpering, in obvious pain. Despite being fourteen years old and her life about to end, I still thought of her as my puppy. I'd gotten her the moment I moved out at eighteen. She'd moved across the country with me, been by my side through two long-term relationships and always offered unconditional support.

The first tear that had welled in my eye rolled down

my cheek as I nodded my consent. The veterinary office was lined with posters for flea control and vet approved food. All featured happy looking animals, so full of life and vigour. There was stark contrast in their appearance to my old and faithful friend. Brandy's grey muzzle and rheumy eyes were painful to compare.

The vet assured me I was making the right decision and that Brandy had no quality of life left. I had to agree. Her life wasn't one of quality; she could barely get up after lying down, not even to go to the toilet. Mostly, she didn't even try anymore and just went on her bed. And yet, she'd still thump her tail every time I walked into the room or approached her. No quality of life, sure. But it was still a life. One I'd just consented to end. Sadness flowed through me and more tears ran down my cheeks.

The vet gave the injection as I lay holding her. In a few moments, Brandy's eyes dilated and her breathing slowed and stopped. Her loyal, affectionate and well-lived life had come to an end. I felt hollow as the finality sunk in.

The vet said she'd give me a few minutes to say goodbye and handed me a specimen jar for her nametag. As she left, I was told to tap on the door when I was ready.

A wave of guilt made me cry even more. 'I'm so sorry,' I sobbed as more tears fell.

I don't know what it was that made me do it, but I

decided to collect my tears in the specimen jar. I think I wanted to quantify my emotion. In some way, I hoped that it would show Brandy's spirit how much I cared for her, how much guilt I felt, and how much her loss was hurting me.

I hugged Brandy closer and repeated, 'I'm so sorry.' As more tears rolled, I collected them in the jar. I took off her collar and slipped it into my pocket. A few minutes later, I tapped on the door.

The Vet appeared a moment later and said that I could leave straight away and they would sort out payment later. I could only nod in reply. I took one last look at my beloved dog and exited the room. I don't remember how I got to the car or starting the drive home, but I know at one point grief overwhelmed me. I just managed to hold myself together long enough to pull over. Tears flowed freely and were collected in the jar.

I realised why the most emotional I'd ever seen my father was when our family dog was put down. It was somehow different with an animal you felt a connection to. Probably the lack of being able to use words to express emotion or share understanding. There was simply a bond that seemed unbreakable until it was abruptly broken.

#

My rented unit seemed empty when I walked in. My

obsessive neatness for everything except Brandy and her toys amplified that something was missing from the house. I half expected to hear the usual heart-warming thump of Brandy's tail as I entered the living area. She always knew when it was me and not my housemate, Timothy. He'd told me he'd be out doing something, but I can't remember what it was. I put the nametag and collar in a drawer and placed the jar of tears on the kitchen bench. There was a few millilitres of fluid in the jar. It seemed such a trivial amount compared to the guilt and grief I felt. How could this sufficiently represent the size of my loss? More tears came, but they added little to the volume collected. Wondering what to do with the tears, I remembered the capsule machine and empty pods a previous tenant had left in the crawlspace in the ceiling. I'd discovered them when I put away some boxes. Finding them had made me wonder if the previous tenant had been a drug dealer, chemist or someone who made their own herbal remedies. I knew I could put the tears into the capsules. At least it would be something to do to distract me for a while.

The pull-down ladder made retrieving the device straightforward. I took it to the kitchen. I'd never used such a machine before. It seemed odd to call it a machine, given that it was only a few pieces of plastic. The base was rectangular, with twelve holes for the capsule bases. I put a few of the bases into the device and carefully poured tears into them. I had never realised before, but the bases ran the length of the capsule. The 'cap' was simply that, a cap that was placed over the top and then 'tamped' into place using the top half of the machine. The size '0' capsules held 0.68ml each which was about 11 tears. I was surprised that I only filled four capsules as it felt like I'd cried a proverbial river.

I was devastated. I felt broken and guilty for agreeing to put Brandy down. I hurt, yet the loss quantified was a mere four capsules of tears? The idea seemed absurd. I packed away the machine and put it in the drawer alongside Brandy's nametag. I wrote a sarcastic, 'to feel better, take two,' on a sheet of paper.

My phone rang. It was Sven. I'd formed a friendship with him after meeting him at the dog park. Even though I'd lived in the city for a year and a half, most of my friends had been made that way. Sven invited me over for coffee and assured me I could cry as much as I wanted without judgement as he'd lost his dog six months ago and knew how I felt.

Brandy hadn't been able to go 'walkies' for months, but the walk Sven's house felt odd without her by my side. I'd only ever walked this way with her.

Near the dog park, a warehouse had been converted into townhouses, one of which was Sven's. He greeted me with a hug and invited me in. Inside, was a large mezzanine level, which was used as Sven and his boyfriend's bedroom. Underneath that was a kitchen and bathroom and the rest was an open plan living area. We went to the back of the property where there was a tiny courtyard. It was good that Sven lived near the park and his dog had been a Jack Russel. Any larger breed would not have fit the space. We sat outside so Sven could smoke. Sven was in his fifties, but had the body of a fitness instructor. He'd been a firefighter before moving into occupational health and safety. His approach to life was that it should be enjoyed. He relished new experiences and travelled often. His worldliness would soon prove useful. Sven kept a clock in the courtyard so he wouldn't spend hours contemplating life without realising the time. I notice it's three o'clock.

I explain what happened with Brandy, emphasising my guilt and remorse. I cry a little bit but, as promised, Sven doesn't make me feel self-conscious. After a while, he responds rhetorically, 'What does it mean to forgive someone? What does it mean to forgive yourself?'

I shrug.

'How do you move on from something that you feel guilty for? What if you've wronged someone?' he said.

'I don't know,' I said realising I really didn't know.

'Someone once described a cultural practice in Zambia. When a tribal member has wronged the group they are forgiven in a special ceremony. The tribe recounts all the positive things the person has done for the group. At the end, the transgressor's place in the society is affirmed and they're accepted back into the tribe. Rumours suggest that the practice has almost died out, as it's so successful in promoting harmony it's no longer needed. I mean think about it, by the end, you'd realise that it's important to have the person in your life and they feel the same about you. You'd have truly forgiven them.'

There was wisdom in Sven's words. This was exactly what I needed from Brandy. A chance to receive forgiveness for putting her to sleep. Sven advised me to go through my role in Brandy's life from her perspective. She must've thought I was ageless— I'd hardly changed while she went through her entire life cycle.

I recall the day she entered my home. I'd just moved away from my parents, but she was more scared than me. I'd slept beside her in the laundry to help her feel safe. My mind saw a montage of the thousands of walks, treats and meals she knew I'd provided. I recall moving to the other side of the country and her flying over to join me. Her excitement at our reunion meant she jumped a metre high fence to get to me. I saw me as her provider, her protector, her friend. I thought of how she'd follow me from room to room, just to be close by. Sometimes, she'd move when I only switched sides of the couch. Through Brandy's eyes, I was an endless source of pats and hugs. Touch was always the way we'd shown our affection.

At bedtime, she'd always come over for a scratch behind the ears and lick of my hand before circling her mat in the corner and flopping with a contented sigh— a nightly ritual that would be no more. I thought of so many instances and events where I brought joy into her life. Maybe I wronged Brandy by putting her to sleep, but she would've understood why. She'd absolve me due to the role I'd had in her life.

A weight lifts from my shoulders. I feel Brandy's spirit forgive me. Sven and I talk about some gossip from the dog park for a while before I head home.

#

When I walked into the kitchen of my unit, my housemate Timothy was there. He was acting strangely for someone who knew what I'd been through. He'd only known Brandy for six months and so always knew she would not be around for much longer, so he never got attached enough to especially mourn her loss, but he seemed…happy? I'd have expected more support from him.

'What was in those pills? They're amazing, I feel so awesome,' Timothy said.

It took me a moment to realise he was talking about the capsules of tears. I was speechless. I attempted to explain what they were, but I couldn't find a way to make the idea seem rational. A thought occurred to me.

'I dunno. What time did you take them?'

'I got home about… so must've been just after three. Why?'

I waved my hand to dismiss the question and left the kitchen. I knew he'd put it down to me being upset over Brandy. The strange thing was I didn't feel so upset anymore. In fact, if I'd estimated it, I'd have said I felt halfway to feeling better. What if by consuming my tears Timothy had taken away the pain that caused them? That could've explained why I felt better. It's said people who practice compassion are happier people. By this logic, if Timothy consuming my tears was responsible for reducing my angst, he should've felt happier too. It seemed to me that it could be so. All I knew was that I'd ask him to take the other two in the morning to see how it would make me feel.

# The Lost Chapter
# Act 1: The Heist

'So I was wondering if you could recommend someone who could steal something for me,' Dr Engels said to his friend Brad Thomas. They were sitting Dr Engel's office at Leviathan Enterprises having one of their occasional catch-ups.

'Err, you do know I'm a Sergeant, right?'

'Yes, that's why I'm asking you.'

'I can't help you steal something.' Brad was incredulous.

'You won't be. That's what I need them for.'

'I can't believe I'm even entertaining this question,

but I'll bite. If I've heard of them then they wouldn't be all that good.'

'Well, can you make some enquiries amongst those you do know?'

'I guess so. What do you want stolen anyway?'

'You know how you asked me if I knew of a way to change the world – to get it back on track?'

Brad mirrored the doctors movements and lent forward in his leather armchair.

'I think I have a way to do it. You remember the Professor?'

Brad nodded and took a sip of his whisky, enjoying the burning sensation the cask strength spirit produced.

'I miss him terribly and I've been thinking a lot lately about his legacy. He was my best friend and I really don't want him to be remembered for the negative side effects of his program, which thankfully you avoided. I'd like to honour him through making his plan to fix the world available, even if we keep it quiet about where it came from. He made it before he created the intelligence raising program you worked through.'

Brad smiled at the memory. He'd gained a lot from the program both professionally and personally.

'So why didn't he use it?'

'For him the challenge was the creation of such a … manifesto. That was what he found interesting—the task of creating it, not its implementation.'

'What happened to it? What was in it?'

'He only mentioned it a couple of times. I think it was written as a chapter for *The Conversationist*— you know that series of themed daydreams he wrote into a book. But he discarded it as it didn't fit with the rest of the book and mixed up the alternating perspectives.'

Brad sighed and rolled his eyes.

'Yes, I'm getting to it. I think what he wrote was a basically a way of uniting people behind a movement, one that would be irresistible due to some factor or factors that he didn't elaborate upon. The copy he told me about is in a safe, err … actually, it's more of a bank vault.'

'Hang on, you want me to get someone to rob a bank for you? I can't do that.'

Dr Engels smiled. 'Well, not the whole bank, just a safety deposit box.'

Brad laughed. 'I don't think that makes it any better, but let's say I find someone and they're able to get to the box. I take it you know what to do with the contents?'

'Getting the manifesto will need to be step one. If we can do that then we'll see if we can use it. For now, we just need to obtain it.'

Brad took a sip of his drink. 'Okay. Because it's you asking, I'll see what I can do. But you have to make sure I never know what comes of any information I give you.'

'Sure, sure. You cannot know about any criminal

activity.'

'But do let me know what's in it.'

Brad finished his drink and drove home slowly to his fiancée. He took numerous side streets so he could contemplate the doctor's request.

#

The next morning Brad walked the streets of the city looking for an informant he knew. He hadn't wandered the city for months. It wasn't a large city, but it still had a blend of old and new buildings and some shadier sections.

Brad was dressed casually and while there was still the chance someone might recognise him, given the publicity he'd received in the last year, he was as anonymous as possible.

After searching for much of the morning Brad found Ryan outside a souvenir shop in London Court: a Tudor themed street, which was little more than a tourist trap.

'Hi Ryan.'

Ryan looked him over.

'I haven't done anything,' he said lacking conviction.

'Okay.'

'What do you want then?'

'How about I buy you a drink?'

Ryan nodded. They walked to one of the street's small, crowded cafés.

Ryan ordered the most expensive drink on the menu.

They stood at the bar, like they were in Italy. The place was so crowded that they had to lean in close to each other to be heard.

'Hypothetically speaking, if I wanted to hire someone to steal something for me who would you recommend?' Brad said amused he was asking the question.

'Let me think about that for a moment and not answer because you're setting me up.'

'I don't believe in entrapment and it's more a case of needing someone to give advice for a friend who's, uh, writing a novel,' Brad lied. 'Do you know anyone or not?'

'What sort of place would they be stealing from? Home, shop, car?'

'Bank.'

'You're freaking kidding me.'

'No. Like I said, it's um, for a novel.'

'I've heard rumours about a consulting thief who likes tricky gigs. I'll see what I can find out and get back to you. By the way if you're setting me up I'll sling a lot of mud in your direction and some of it will stick.'

'I know that, which is why you can be confident this won't be on the record.'

'So, how do I get the information to you?'

'How about we meet back here tomorrow.'

'How about I give you a call instead. I can be seen with you once, but twice in short succession is not good for business.'

Brad handed him his business card and quickly returned to the station.

#

'Hi Sergeant, I have the name for you. You need to talk to Jimmy 'Mug' Punter. He usually hangs out at Bacchus Bar. You'll need to tell him the phrase, 'Only the foolhardy would embark on such a quest', at some point when you or your friend meet him.'

'Thanks.'

'By the way, everyone knows he's dyslexic but him. He mixed up my phone number the first time I tried to have him call me and I had to use a few IOUs to get his number, so you owe me at least one.'

'Okay. How about I use my discretion for your next misdemeanour.'

'Hey, that's insulting. How do you know I'll do something wrong again?'

'Am I wrong?'

'That's not the point.'

They laughed.

'Speak soon,' Ryan said as he hung up. Brad smiled at Ryan potentially meaning he was about to break the law.

#

Jimmy 'Mug' Punter was sitting in his usual booth in Bacchus Bar. The bar was modelled on the quintessential

British Pub and was designed to allow conversations. Mug's booth had walls on three sides and was informally reserved for him between the hours of 5pm and 9pm, Tuesday to Thursday.

Mug sat opposite his new acquaintance, who appeared to be viewing him with a mixture of curiosity and admiration. Mug knew that despite his small frame, grey hair and world-weary stare, he was in great shape and radiated health.

'I was wondering if I could interest you in a job?' Dr Engels asked.

'Yeah?'

'Only the foolhardy would embark on such a quest.'

'Really?'

'So I'm told.'

'By who?'

'By whom, and the answer is Ryan.'

'How do you know him?'

'I don't, he's the friend of a friend.'

'Hmm,' Mug said thoughtfully. He studied the doctor's face and wondered if he was being set-up. There seemed to be something familiar about him.

'Who do you work for?'

'Leviathan Enterprises.'

'You're that doctor. The one involved in the intelligence raising thingy.'

'Yes.'

'Hmm,' Mug mumbled again. 'Okay, let's talk about a job, but only hypothetically. Maybe imagine how it might be done.'

Dr Engels smiled.

'I was imagining there may be an item in the safety deposit box of a deceased friend that I'd like to retrieve. The bank would be in the oldest part of the city and have an underground vault. I believe I can imagine a way for you to steal the item without needing to set foot in the vault and without having to override the bank's security. I imagine that if this is done correctly, the bank will not know anything's been taken for another fifty-three years when the lease on the box expires. Ideally they might even think the box was meant to be empty. We'd want this to be as discreet as possible.'

Mug nodded. 'You said you have a plan, so how do you imagine doing it?'

'The most important thing to know is that I own the safety deposit box next to the one I'd want you to steal from. We got them together a long time ago.'

'Kind of a couples thing?' Mug asked curiously.

'While I had great affection for the Professor, he was not that way inclined, so nothing like that. It's more a case of our younger selves deciding having a safety deposit box would make us important, then going to the bank together to get them.'

'Okay.'

Dr Engels explained how he'd like Mug to steal the safe from the vault and why he thought it the plan would work.

'No. Way,' Mug said. 'Deal's off.'

'I'll make it worth your while.'

'I'm not sure any amount of money is worth that.'

'How about a fifty grand for the person who does the cutting and forty each for two accomplices.'

'No,' Mug said firmly. 'How would you afford that anyway? Are you a billionaire?'

'Not this year,' Dr Engel's sighed. 'My best offer is seventy to the cutter and sixty to each of the others.'

'Best offer?' Mug queried, annoyed at the tone of temptation appearing in his voice.

'Best offer.'

'I'll think about it. What about expenses?'

'At your expense, but if you wind up needing a lawyer or medical, I'll cover that as an extra payment.'

'Hmm.' Mug was lost in thought, 'I'll call the lads and let you know,' he eventually replied.

#

The next evening Mug was joined in his booth by his colleagues. 'Murky' Thomas was his driver and lookout and Slavish McReedy was his gadget guy and safe cracker.

'What's up?' asked Slavish.

'We've got a job.'

'We know. You called us here to discuss it,' said Murky with a grin.

Mug ignored him. 'The target is the contents of a safety deposit box from a bank vault. If we can get it, it's worth either sixty grand each or seventy if you take the main role.'

'That's not how we work Mug, you know that,' Murky said. 'Besides, I need more money for Annie's medical expenses.'

Slavish tilted his head sideways. 'I know you wouldn't even put the idea of different payments to us unless there was a reason, so what is it?'

Mug explained the plan.

'I take it back,' Murky said. 'It's all yours.'

'Yep,' Slavish agreed.

'I was hoping you would take the opportunity Murky, and put your hand up for the extra. What with your daughter and all.'

'No. Annie's stable enough that sixty will suit me just fine.'

'I'll guess I'll have to do it,' Mug said grudgingly. 'Slavish, can you get me some gear for protection?'

Slavish grinned. 'Sure.'

Mug knew this caper was not going to be the usual amount of fun for him.

Dr Engels had provided centimetre perfect details of where they'd need to be and he'd even given them a positioning tracker and a high powered laser cutter to assist with the theft. They were pleased to have two months to finesse the finer details of the plan, especially since they'd be executing it on a Friday while the bank was open.

#

Nearly two months later, Murky drove Mug and Slavish close to the target bank. Dr Engels had used a contact at the Department of Infrastructure to get Murky a job there and Murky had completed his orientation training and first few solo jobs. Dr Engels had hacked into the department's intranet, raised a work order and assigned Murky as the technician for it, thus Murky was driving a department vehicle and had proper documentation for the job.

'It's better if you hide something in plain sight,' Dr Engels had said to Mug when discussing why all the subterfuge was necessary. 'Making all the supporting resources genuine will make the crime better concealed and harder to detect. Plus Murky can work for a couple of weeks or whatever is necessary and then quit saying the job wasn't for him.'

In Mug's experience people never questioned whether workmen had a right to be in a certain place. However, Dr Engels insisted on the extra level of precaution and since he was paying Mug agreed.

Mug watched Murky from the van as Murky set-up

witches hats and a yellow painted metal fence around a manhole that was near the intersection of a dead-end laneway and a main road. They were a hundred metres from the bank. Murky placed several signs on the metal fence to warn people to mind their step.

Mug got out of the van. He was dressed in a disposable white coverall and he held a gas mask that Slavish had designed. The gas mask would cover his face and fit neatly within the hood of the coverall. Mug put it on as Slavish gave him some advice.

'The coveralls will stop your skin coming into contact with the sludge. You won't be exposed to anything really toxic. Remember the mask is mostly to filter out the smell and airborne viruses or bacteria, so you should be okay. Still, I'm glad it's you and not me.'

'I can't believe I'm about to go crawling through a sewer.'

'Yeah, it's a shit job but somebody's got to do it,' Murky chimed in. Mug laughed despite himself.

Murky used a crowbar to lift the cover off the access pipe. Mug gagged as he descended the ladder and again when he stepped in something.

'That feels so wrong. It's like treading on the world's largest dog poo.'

'Except it's human,' Slavish said, sounding cheerful.

'You're not helping.'

'Who said I was here to help?'

'Remind me to cut you out of the next job.'

'Sure, but before you do that there's something you should know.'

'What's that?'

'That mask uses active filtering.'

'So?'

'Limited battery life. Unless you want to know what a thousand bowel motions smells like you'd better get moving.'

Mug grimaced and lowered himself further into the sludge. The pipe was only just wider than Mug. He turned on the light that was built into the mask and immediately turned it off again. It was better not to look at that. He began crawling commando style towards their target. It took him nearly four minutes, partly due to the narrowness of the pipe, but mostly because he kept trying to hold himself and the bucket he was carrying out of the sludge.

Dr Engels had placed a short-range tracking device in his safety Deposit box that would let Mug know when he was at the right place. Once Mug was within a meter of the target at the bank, he turned the light on and took out the laser cutter. The cutter had several advantages: it was very quiet, produced little waste—as most of the material would be vaporised by the cutter—and it cut cleanly making repairs easy. It was connected via a long cord to a power pack in the van. The cord also circulated coolant to prevent the device overheating.

Mug pressed a button on his mask that switched it to welding mode. The glass shield turned translucent. The laser itself was colourless, but when it cut the inch thick concrete wall of the sewer it produced a bright flame. Mug cut a hole, the size and shape of a laptop into the side of the pipe. He removed and carefully placed the section of pipe next to him, pleased it had remained in one piece. Fresh from his training, Murky had told Mug he wasn't allowed to use a hammer and chisel as it would make repairs too difficult.

Mug scooped sandy soil from inside the hole into a bucket he'd brought with him, knowing the soil would have to be replaced before he left.

'Uh, Houston. We have a problem.'

'What do you mean?' asked Murky.

'The bucket isn't big enough for all the dirt.'

'Well put the excess next to it.'

'You realise that means I'll have to… I'll have to scoop up some of the sewerage.'

'So?'

'With my hands.'

'You have gloves.'

'Still not okay. Ahhh,' Mug yelled.

'Settle down, it's not that bad.'

'No that's not it— a rat just ran over me.'

Murky and Slavish burst out laughing.

Mug shook his head. 'Sometimes you guys are not good friends.'

'Yeah, we know,' Murky said sounding cheerful.

'Ooh,' Mug said.

'What is it this time?' Slavish asked.

'I've reached the bricks of the bank. This really is an old building.'

Mug removed more dirt until he'd exposed some brickwork. Nearly a century of temperature fluctuations, water and general deterioration, had led what remained of the grout to be crumbly. It took Mug a short time to gouge out the grout and remove three columns of three bricks. He shone his light into the hole and was nearly blinded by the reflection from a sheet of metal, which was between the wall and the safety deposit boxes. He pressed another button on his mask, which made the visor turn nearly opaque. He took out the laser cutter again. The steel sheet came away readily. Mug turned off the cutter and changed the visor back to clear. He'd exposed six rectangles on the back of the safety deposit boxes, indicating the size and location of each box. Mug's tracker locator's light turned from red to green when he placed it on the middle of the top row. That was the doctor's box.

'I need the one to the left of the doc's right?'

'Left is right, right is wrong. Gottit?' asked Slavish.

'Don't mix them up like you usually do,' Murky

chimed in.

'You guys suck. I was just double checking.'

Mug held his hands up with his palms facing down. His thumb and first finger on his left hand formed an 'L' shape. 'Left,' he whispered to himself.

Mug drew an 'X' on the box they wanted and switched his equipment back to cutting mode. A few moments later and he'd cut around the outline of the Professor's Safety deposit box. He removed the piece of metal and reached in to retrieve their target.

'Hmph,' Mug grunted.

'What?' Murky asked.

'It looks like it's just a block of aluminium. I can't see how it could contain anything or how you'd open it.'

'You're sure you have the right box?'

Mug checked again. 'Yes.'

'Okay, well patch up the safe, wall and pipe and hurry back,' Slavish said.

#

Twenty minutes later Mug was crawling backwards towards the manhole.

'Get the hose ready.'

'Don't worry, it is; we don't want to be smelling you all the way back to base.' Mug had been amused when he saw the shower for the first time. It was like those he'd seen in disaster movies about a chemical or biological hazard.

When Mug emerged from the hole, Murky and Slavish burst out laughing. Mug knew that even his upper back and head were covered in sewage. He laughed when the scent hit them a moment later and their laughter turned to gagging.

'Quick get him in the shower,' Murky implored Slavish. Slavish pointed Mug to the shower tent they'd set up. Mug kept the mask on while he let the water run over him. He watched brown water run straight towards the manhole from which he'd just emerged. Three minutes later, Mug turned off the shower and stripped off the coveralls. He wrapped them in three plastic bags and put them in a lidded bucket. Only then did he take off the mask. Mug was left wearing a singlet and shorts.

'I hope you repaired the pipe properly, otherwise that vault is going to smell,' Slavish said as mug exited the tent.

'I did, I know the stakes, so don't worry I took my time and repaired everything properly.'

'How soon can we incinerate this?' Mug asked, handing Murky the bucket.

'I'll do it back at the depot.'

'Look at you all workmanlike. I never thought I'd hear you talking about a proper job like it was normal for you,' Mug said.

'Yeah, well maybe I'm liking the idea of regular income and the way Annie is looking at me these days.

Plus not feeling like I'm waiting for the law to catch up to me.' Murky said.

'Uh, we did just rob a bank,' Slavish reminded him.

'Yeah, but … um, you know what just let it go. Let's clear up this area. I knock off at three, so let's meet back at the Doc's place at four,' Murky said.

'Okay,' Mug and Slavish replied.

#

At 4.03pm the security guard who controlled who the lift to the offices of Dr Engel's company, Leviathan Enterprises, watched three out of place characters walk towards him. The doctor had advised him they'd be coming, but it was still an odd sight to see the trio approach. They walked with a slight hesitancy that the guard only noticed due to his time in drama school when they'd covered movement as a means of displaying character. He let the trio up with a curt nod.

#

Dr Engels greeted them as they exited the elevator. 'Gentlemen, welcome.'

'Errr, thanks?' Mug mumbled on behalf of the trio.

'Normally I'd have my assistant offer guests a coffee, but you boys look like you could use a drink. What'll it be? Beer? Whisky?

'Beer,' Murky and Slavish said without hesitancy.

'Whisky, please. With cola,' Mug said. He watched Dr Engels' eye twitch as he spun on his heels to go and fix the drinks.

'Whad'you think about these digs boys?' Mug asked, looking around at the spotless and modern design of the office. Light filled every room and even the hallways due to clever use of mirrors and the floor to ceiling windows.

'I've never seen the city from this far up,' Murky said.

'Are you okay Murk? You look a little seasick,' Mug teased. 'Perhaps you should back away from the window?'

'I'll be right when I get that beer.'

They looked expectantly towards the anteroom the Doctor had gone into.

'Guess we'll just have to wait a bit longer. In the meantime, you guys think we should…'

Slavish stopped as Dr Engels reappeared carrying a tray with two beers, a whisky and cola and a straight whisky. He handed the drinks to his guests.

'Thanks Doc,' each said in turn.

Slavish's phone rang. 'Uh, 'scuse me. It's my girlfr…' He wandered off towards the elevator and Dr Engels led the others to a small room with a horseshoe of two-seater sofas with glass coffee tables next to each arm.

#

'Gentlemen, I don't know if you know Sergeant Thomas?' Dr Engels asked as he introduced them to a man who was already sipping a whisky and sitting on one of the sofas. He put down the glass and stood.

184

'What's this?' Mug asked, 'You setting us up?'

Dr Engel's watched Mug's face darken. He suddenly felt like he was in danger. Mug looked like he knew how to handle himself.

'No, no. Sorry, I've known Brad for years and his contact recommended you to me. I should have chosen my words more carefully. He's here to help, not to arrest you.'

'Yes and on that note, please don't say anything about how you obtained whatever's in that bag. That would place me in an awkward position,' Brad said, sounding genial.

'Speaking of which, may I have the item?' Dr Engels asked.

Dr Engels watched Mug reach into his bag and pulled out the object. He handed it over to the doctor. Dr Engels looked at the thin metal slab like it was a puppy who'd returned after going missing. A moment later he felt the colour drain from his face. It seemed he wouldn't be able to honour his friend after all. Dr Engels felt a tear well in his eye. 'I'm afraid this has all been for nothing.'

'We still get paid right?' Mug asked.

'The safe is one I designed a decade ago. It can't be opened.' Dr Engels slumped onto a sofa. The others followed suit.

'I can't open it … You see, it's meant to house

something that would not need to be accessed in a hurry and would be destroyed if someone tried to break into it. Think of it as a high-tech update on a cryptex. The way you access it is rather unique and unfortunately in this instance, impossible without a computer file that no longer exists.'

'But you do impossible things quite regularly. Why can't you open it? Surely you'd have some means,' Brad said.

'No.'

'What about your network of free thinkers?'

'No, not even they could help.'

'Really?'

'Yes. I'm afraid so.' Dr Engels sat and took a large sip of whisky.

'So after all this setup we're not going to find out what was the Professor's plan to get the world back on track?'

'I guess not.'

Dr Engels looked up as Slavish came bounding into the room. 'I'm going to get lu... wait what happened? Why's everyone so down?'

Mug glanced at Brad. 'Seems we procured a safe we can't get into.'

Slavish looked at the doctor. 'Why?'

'Because I designed it.' Dr Engels voice was slightly hoarse.

'Then tell me about it. Maybe I can get into it for you?'

Dr Engels smiled benignly. 'The safe is a solid piece of 3D printed aluminium, except that in the middle is a copper wire net which houses a document. The wires are connected to a battery that will last nineteen years. Drilling or opening the safe incorrectly will kill the current. It's attached to the electrically conductive paper which contains a reactive ink that will permanently erase if the current is stopped. In order to get to the paper safely you need the 3D printer that made it, which I have, and a computer file, which I don't. The printer then uses high strength acid in lieu of ink and a specialised laser to heat the surface of the safe to 180ºC as the acid is applied. This vaporises the salt that gets produced. The hydrogen gas that's generated is flammable so the printer is encased in what amounts to a fume cupboard that filters the gas and vaporised salts. The laser needs to be precise as the paper will ignite if its temperature reaches 230ºC. There are also some hidden optical fibres which could transmit the laser to the paper and ignite it, as well as, some tiny, magnetic iron bars built in so you can't use an MRI to analyse the safe and x-rays won't penetrate the surface. In short you definitely need the computer file to get in. That file was on the Professor's computer.

'Don't I have that in storage?' Brad asked, recalling

that when the Professor died, the police department had seized his computer as evidence.

'No. That was his latest one. His uni updated their laptops every three years and this,' he held up the safe, 'must be at least ten years old. I'm afraid this has all been for nothing.'

'Do you still have the blueprints?' Slavish asked.

'Yes'

'Could I look at them please?'

Dr Engels started to say no, but with a loud sigh resigned himself to his fate. It's for the professor. He nodded and disappeared down a long corridor. A minute later he returned with a green folder labelled 'XSS-07.' Inside was a sheaf of paper. Slavish flicked through the pages. Whenever a diagram appeared his flicking stopped and he studied the page intensely. Every so often he'd look up at the safe and back to the page.

'Can I have a pencil and paper?'

Dr Engels nodded and quickly went to get them while Slavish continued his reading. When he returned Slavish stopped to jot down some notes.

'So, doctor about my earlier question?' Mug queried. Dr Engels felt his eyes move left as he mentally replayed their conversation.

'Ah yes, payment. Of course you do. Why wouldn't you?'

'I've been dudded before when things haven't been

exactly right.'

'You didn't mention the attachment,' Slavish muttered.

'I don't operate like that, Mug,' Dr. Engels replied, ignoring Slavish.

'It's a shame that the Professor used my design. I didn't think this was what he borrowed the device for. He said it was for a family heirloom.'

'Well it kind of was—' Brad said.

'You said you designed it,' Slavish interjected.

'Yes,' replied the Doctor.

'I take it your background is in biochemistry.'

'Yes. Why?'

'Never get an organic chemist to do an inorganic job.'

'What do you mean?'

'I can get into the safe for you.'

'Really?' Dr Engels was incredulous. 'How?'

'Simple.'

'Perhaps I didn't make myself clear about the design?'

'You did, but you're wrong. LME will save us.'

'And who is that?'

'Exactly my point. You should say what is that? Give me the safe and I'll have it ready to open in, uh … three days, once I've got some supplies.'

Dr Engels felt his face twitch with expressions that alternated between affection for his design, disgust that he couldn't get into it, and frustration someone else potentially could. With a loud sigh he handed the safe to Slavish.

'Fine. Do what you can.'

'Well boys, I'd better get going. I need to get to a supply place before they close at five. I'll see you on Monday.'

'I have work on Monday,' Murky said.

'You're keeping the job?' Mug asked.

'Yes. I kinda like it, and the dependable income is good for dealing with Annie's expenses. When I took her home from school before coming here, she was so excited to show my hi-vis workwear to her friends. She was showing me off to them. How can I stop when she does that?'

'Well look at you taking responsibility. Kudos,' Mug said.

'Fine, make it Tuesday at six. Mug you'll need to let them know where the lab is,' Slavish said.

Dr Engels watched Mug raise an eyebrow. 'You're letting them see your lab?'

Slavish looked around. 'Sure, why not. Later boys.'

'Hang on we'll come too,' Mug replied. He and Murky sculled their drinks and Dr Engels escorted the trio to the elevator.

When they'd left Dr Engels turned to Brad. 'I can't believe I'm trusting a criminal with that.'

'I've met a lot of criminals. They seem different. More noble somehow.'

'Hmm, yes. I think I agree with you. I think it's that they aren't about crime for crime's sake. They want a purpose,' Dr Engels said.

'I think you're right. It's been a most interesting day off. I'll make sure I get to this lab place by six next Tuesday. I can't wait to see what he comes up with.'

#

'Do you see the padlock connecting the garage door to the pavement? Clearly not used for cars,' Brad said to Dr Engels as they walked up the driveway of an inner suburban house. They were guided through a side door by Mug and Murky.

'Gentlemen, welcome to my lab.' Slavish proudly waved his arms around the large garage. Brad saw it was filled with equipment, yet every piece had a place, which led to a neat appearance and room to build things. In the centre of the floor space, atop wooden planks were two industrial fans connected to funnels. Hanging between the funnels and above a small bin filled with polystyrene beads, were two clamps, each with rubber tubing attached to cushion the clamp head. Slavish had set up a chair in each of the corners of the garage. He handed everyone a beer and motioned for them to take a seat. Without hesitation, he launched into his presentation.

'Last week I asked Dr Engels about LME. Today it

will enable us to open the safe. LME is liquid metal embrittlement and it is awesome. The principle is simple; certain metals react with each other to alter the lattice the atoms form when they bind with each other. This means that if enough of the metal is altered its usual properties change. In short, the metal becomes brittle.'

Brad glanced round the room. Only Dr Engels looked like he was following the discussion, which Slavish also seemed to notice. 'That means it becomes crumbly.' Brad felt his expression clear with the sudden understanding.

'On Friday I picked up two kilos of gallium from a school supply outlet. Gallium is a metal that's reasonably dense, so this was a volume of about 340ml, just enough for what we needed it for. I melted it, took the safe and placed it in a plastic tray and coated it in the gallium. I then put it in this egg incubator at 37°C for the last three days. This was warm enough to keep the gallium metal liquid.'

'I thought mercury was the only liquid metal,' Brad said.

'At room temp, yes, but at body temperature, no. Gallium is a metal that will melt in your hand.'

Brad watched Slavish open the incubator and take out the tray. He cautiously lifted the safe out of the silvery liquid and gently swiped the remaining droplets into the tray.

'Don't you need gloves?' Brad asked.

'It's gallium, not mercury. That's why I could get it so easily. It's not toxic,' Slavish said as he carefully put the safe into the clamps. 'So as I was saying the gallium reacts with the aluminium to make the metal crumbly. In a moment I'll use a speaker driver to make the safe fall apart. When I do so, the air current that I'll make with these fans will create a region of low pressure on either side of the safe. The relatively high pressure from within the safe will force the shattering parts of the safe outwards – like an explosion without explosives. And one that won't damage the paper inside.' He grinned.

'To make the safe explode I'll generate its resonance tone at high amplitude. This'll make the whole safe shake rather than just a small part of it and because it'll be brittle it should shatter. All the optical fibres, iron filings and aluminium that protects the paper will be literally blown away. The paper inside its shell of wires will be untouched. We can then either use insulated pliers to prize apart the wires without stopping the current, or depending on what's in there, just read it through the gaps.'

'Wow,' Dr Engels said, 'just brilliant.' Brad looked at the doctor in amusement. He'd never heard him give anyone such high praise. 'I could use someone like you. Would you like a job?' Dr Engels asked.

'I have one.'

'Consultant thief is hardly a job.'

'Yeah but it pays the bills, lets me create the kind of gadgets I daydream about and gives me freedom to do whatever I want.'

'So it fulfils you, I get that. I'd offer you that opportunity too, pay you well and you wouldn't have to break the law at regular intervals.'

Brad thought it would be only irregular ones.

'This may seem like an impromptu offer. It's not. I'd pretty much decided to offer you a job if you could get into the safe, so please consider it.'

'It's tempting, I'll think about it. But let's prove that it'll work first.'

Slavish circled the room and gave each person a pair of safety glasses. 'It shouldn't be forceful, they're just in case.'

Slavish turned on the fans. Brad was sure he saw the safe bulge outwards. Slavish put on a pair of thick gloves and safety glasses. He picked up the speaker driver and flicked a switch on a tone generator. A high pitched squeal could be heard above the sound of the fans. Slavish held the speaker at arm's length and approached the safe.

'I experimented over the weekend and yesterday, so I know this tone will work. Are you guys ready?'

'Yes!' they chorused.

'Here' goes.'

Brad watched as Slavish touched the speaker to the safe. It immediately exploded into thousands of shards the size of grains of sand. As promised the shards flew away from the safe. A copper net dropped into the bin of polystyrene beads.

'Yes!' Dr Engels cried. Brad had never seen him so excited.

They all leapt from their chairs and raced to the bin. Dr Engels reached in and lifted out their prize. Inside the copper net was a single piece of the special paper that had text set out on both sides in two landscape columns. Dr Engels quickly took photos of both sides of the page. Slavish turned off the fans and speaker.

'Doc, I uh, know you want to go read that, but I, uh think I'll take you up on your offer. I think you'll be able to challenge me in way these guys can't.'

'Excellent,' Dr Engels said sounding absent.

'Really?' said Mug.

'What can I say, Murky's inspired me.'

Murky blushed. Brad smiled. 'Two less crims for me to deal with and I didn't even have to make an arrest.'

'Hey. We're consultants not criminals. And who said we'd stop doing our extracurricular activities? We may just cut down a bit. Besides, most of the time what we do would never be reported,' Slavish said.

'True. You guys were not on my radar before this,' Brad said with a laugh. 'Don't worry, you won't be now either.'

'How about we just read the lost chapter?' Dr Engels said quietly. Brad mused that the doctor really did want to honour his friend.

# Intermission:
# Second Constant

The second thing you're not supposed to talk about at dinner parties is politics. I've often wondered why, but assume it's something to do with the problem of encountering someone with different views to your own and starting arguments—often ones that exclude rationality. To me, being able to clearly enunciate a political perspective, an ideology, is a way of cementing your personality and social perspectives and should be something that's celebrated, regardless of your political persuasion. Not being aware of the nature of politics or its role in shaping your life is, to me, a path to an ineffective life.

Sera and I have been living together for a couple of months now, but this topic hasn't come up in our relationship to date. I'd be amazed if her beliefs were exactly like mine, since we had different upbringings. I'd been thinking a lot about this when, one lazy Saturday afternoon, Sera handed me a coffee, sat down opposite me on the couch and asked, 'So Michael, what are your political beliefs?'

'I've been considering this a lot in the last few months, so forgive me if I give a lengthy answer,' I say with a smile.

As she rolls her eyes at me, I can almost read her mind saying, 'What, you overthink something?' She nods her permission even if she had the thought.

'My political beliefs stem from the central perspective that education and health should be free. This immediately puts me on the left of the spectrum, even though I think such assignations as left or right are meaningless, since to me the spectrum is spherical at best. Anyway, I believe that education and health are rights and have held this view for a long time. Recently though, I've had a shift – not from this belief but of my understanding as to why I believe this. Previously, I thought education should be free because I've gained a lot from education and have a vested interest in having more people attend university due to my lecturing job.

'Similarly for health, I've been sick in my life and needed treatment. To me it seems unfair that access is based on who can pay rather than need. But I kept thinking about this and why these two things? Why education and health and why not public transport or guaranteed employment or some other thing? My answer was that these two things are what most prevent people from being active members of society. If you're uneducated then your ability to participate and be useful is reduced, and if you are unwell then the same thing is true. Being me, I couldn't leave it there though. So what? I asked myself. So what if some people can't participate in society. Why should that bother me?'

Sera leans forward a little.

'Well, I answered, I know how I've felt when I've been excluded and I don't want others to feel that way, but more than that, I don't want to live in a society that says that excluding people is okay. I mean think about the poor, the weak, the elderly, the young and so on. If you exclude any of their voices from the public discourse then you cannot have a true democracy. You cannot have a true community dialogue.'

'And so I reached the conclusion that what I really want is to live in an inclusive society and this is kind of my new core belief because it supersedes the others.'

'A world like this, with an open exchange of information amongst people, scientists and innovators would be interesting to see. Imagine the progress we could make as a society and as a species if we all worked together. Such advances would benefit everyone and enable us to overcome some of the largest challenges we face, such as population growth, the environment, food, health and welfare. But it'd also mean huge technological advances and potentially interplanetary colonisation. And of course this is linked to evolution.'

Sera rolls her eyes at me again. 'Must you always relate things to that?' she asks with an amused yet sarcastic look.

'What's wrong with that? It's an important idea.'

'But you harp on about it sooo much.'

'I do. But you love me so you'll just have to resign yourself to the fact that you'll hear about it from time to time.'

'Yes I do love you …' Sera trails off, deliberately letting her sentence seem conditional.

I decide to ignore her baiting of me due her looking her most beautiful when she's being playful.

'If you think about evolution as being survival of the fittest, then an inclusive society will benefit the species since you get a wider gene pool, better survival rates due to community support and access to care, and more competition for mating partners which brings about a selection pressure that drives change in the species. The thing is though, promoting the evolutionary benefits of an inclusive society should help draw people to the idea. If people are aware that such a society improves humans as a species, then that should be appealing. I mean it should have an intrinsic value for people.'

'That's an interesting idea, but you're overlooking something.'

'What's that?'

'Well, and this is curious, such a selection pressure also comes from an excluding society. The exclusion also makes for increased competition between people and therefore increases the selection pressure that drives evolution.'

'I'd considered that, but that's not ideal as such a society also drives division between people and therefore misses out on the benefits of inclusion such as the exchange of ideas and drive for betterment and ultimately the diversity of the species. Plus, diversity in the gene pool strengthens the species.'

'Hmph,' Sera grunts as she considers the idea, 'So, what about the marketplace?'

'Inclusivity does't say anything about the free market or locus of control of production, it's more about participation. So you could have an inclusive free market or an inclusive centralised or government controlled market.'

'So are you really trying to say that this could work in any country?'

'Yes, I suppose so.'

'So it's really your plan for world domination,' Sera says with a smile.

'It could be, so I guess so.'

'How would you go about it?'

'I suppose I could form a political party and campaign around this. At least I'd be able to outline a clear vision for the country— unlike our current politicians. Quite simple really…' I stand and start speaking like I'm at a campaign rally. 'I would like to see our country become one which is inclusive so that people are able to contribute to society.' I sit back down.

'There would be no need to define on what basis such as regardless of creed, colour etcetera, because there is no need to qualify the statement, which keeps it simple and easy to communicate. The party could have a framework like some businesses do – a vision, mission, values and objectives policy.' I stand back up again.

'Our Vision: a society where everyone is included and has an opportunity to lead a productive and fulfilling life. Our Mission: to bring about such a society. Our Values: would naturally spring from this such as collaboration, simplicity, inclusion and innovation. Our Objectives and Policies would also relate to this. For example, free education and free health. The beauty of such a framework is that it would also act as a filter for decision making so members of the party would know how to respond to curly questions, even if there was no formalised objective for them.'

'Curly questions such as?'

'How do you feel about abortion? I mean that's usually a big deal.'

'How would they respond to that?'

'All they'd have to do is consider how their response fits with the vision and mission statements. Which means that their response would be along the lines of, yes in the case of rape or medical grounds. Yes, if continuing the pregnancy would ruin a person's life. No to late term terminations except on medical grounds.'

'What about public transport?'

'Yes as it gives people the opportunity to travel for employment, leisure and access to services. This increases inclusion.'

'What about border protection?'

'Again all you have to do is think about what would be the inclusive policy. Inclusivity isn't necessarily the more the merrier and you have to have a process for immigration, even on humanitarian grounds. Similarly, if you consider the vision, then you don't want people to feel excluded from this country. If it were completely open borders, then that would actually not be inclusive because you couldn't track the immigrants or work out where resources are needed and you may make the rest of the population feel undervalued. So the policy wouldn't be come one come all, but would be apply and we'll process your application as quickly as possible. If you're a humanitarian applicant then we'll house you and look after you until you can be processed.'

'What about marriage equality?'

'That one's easy – yes the party would be for it. Next!' I say knowing Sera shares this view.

'What about mining?'

'We need the products of mining in pretty much every aspect of our lives, so yes the party would be for that, but only in areas where people wouldn't be displaced and after the mine closes the area would have to be rehabilitated. If there's a mining camp left behind then the facilities could be used for education, community housing etcetera.'

'Paid maternity leave.'

'Absolutely. Otherwise you make it harder for women in the workplace. Plus if you apply the vision and think about how inclusivity could be increased with such a policy then you would want that to be government funded so that the burden wouldn't be on employers – otherwise they may exclude women.'

'I see. I do like how you could work out a stance on most political issues simply by running it through the vision and mission filter. What you're already achieving is a cohesive set of party policies. Think about what that would mean for how such a party, especially if it was in power, would communicate with people. It would be revolutionary, mostly because it would be upfront. Most parties try to obscure their ideology, yours wouldn't.'

I love it when Sera latches onto one of my ideas and takes it further than I have or could have on my own. She always seems so alive in these moments and it's at these times when I feel my strongest love for her.

'Explain.'

'Well, even a layperson could understand how a policy was created, but more than that; if a decision was made, even if they weren't involved with the process, they could understand how it was made and more importantly, why. That's not something you'd normally get with politics and it would be amazing. I mean, I would vote for such a party in a heartbeat.'

I smile at her comment.

'It's a very holistic philosophy too. I mean you appeal to the biological through the link to evolution, the psychological through the thoughts about the improvement of the species and the social through the betterment of society and social harmony.'

'Yes, when you put it like that it certainly is. Kudos to me.' I say while attempting to pat myself on the back. Unfortunately, I'm not very flexible so this doesn't look quite the way I expect.

Sera laughs and then becomes more serious.

'Are you going to put it into practice?' she asks.

'No.'

'Why not?'

'That's not for me. I'm an armchair thinker, a daydreamer for whom it's more about working out how something could be done rather than the doing of it. I'm a philosopher not a politician,' I say, suddenly realising how pompous I sound. Sera, thankfully, lets me get away with this.

'Maybe you could pass on the idea to someone who could run with it?'

'I've thought about that and yes I could, but despite what I see as an elegant and beautiful way of making decisions and driving the country forward, I'm not sure how it practical it is in our two-party system. However, I do think it would be a uniting vision and one that people would rally behind.'

'Indeed.'

'But also there is a more concrete reason… I don't want people to simply clone or copy my beliefs but to work out what matters to them. That's the wonder of politics—it can tell you what you value, believe and want. Sorting this out for yourself is what I believe is important. So, rather than have me lead a push for this kind of policy, I want to see it occur organically within people. Who knows maybe one day I'll come up with a way to raise people's awareness so that they would push for such a party all by themselves.'

'Ooh that sounds like a cool idea. How would you do that?'

'I haven't thought about it before, so I don't know.'

'I like the idea of getting society to a critical mass of awareness where they seek out inclusivity for themselves. So go on, off the top of your head, what would you put in such a program?'

'Hmm, well it would have to be graduated with distinct steps. I mean you would have to have … levels, for want of a better word. You'd need to make people aware of the major driving forces in society such as ideology and evolution.'

Sera raises an eyebrow and laughs. 'Evolution again! Give it a rest.'

'Fine, I need to get some other notes,' I say, fighting the urge the hit her with a cushion. 'But that's what sprang to mind. Look how about I worry about that later?' I realise I was about to say after our honeymoon and smile to myself that I'm thinking this way about her.

'I think that program, should be your priority. It would be fascinating,' Sera says earnestly.

'I'm afraid it can't be,' I say with mock mournfulness.

'Why not?'

'Well, my dear, you're my priority,' I say with a smirk.

'Good answer,' she says before coming over and straddling me for long kiss, 'Now show me.'

I love the way stimulating Sera's mind turns her on.

I forget about philosophy and give in to the most basic
of evolved behaviours—lust.

# Act 2: Change the World

Act 2 has not been written. The world is not going to change itself. That is up to you.

# Devilish Tricks

Casimir Hendrix paused to take some deep breaths. He was hiking the trail of a 'Thousand Steps' to the top of One Tree Hill. It was arduous despite it being a common track for fitness buffs and people who enjoyed the bushland the track wound through. The ferns and trees which lined the path always seemed to be lush, even in the summer. Today, the misty air betrayed the late winter. Casimir grinned at his exertion. After all, some effort should be required when part of you is seeking the Devil. A hundred and fifty years ago, One Tree Hill had been cleared leaving a single tree, giving rise to its name. Now, it's name was betrayed by thousands of trees that filled the area.

The picnic ground near the top of the steps was an open area with a few wooden tables, a brick barbeque, and a corrugated iron covered shelter. It was deserted on the cold morning. Despite not really having a form, the red blur with black flecks was still recognisable as the Devil; who stood out sitting on top of a table. The Devil didn't seem to be doing anything in particular, which made Casimir wonder if he was waiting for himself. Casimir was surprised at how boldly he approached the figure. He'd long thought about what he'd ask of the Devil should the opportunity arise, and had even formulated a plan to trick him into something miraculous. However, after the long hike he was starving, so he was almost willing to give away the trick in exchange for some breakfast.

The Devil spoke as Casimir approached. 'You're not afraid?' The top of the blur twisted like a dog when it doesn't understanding something.

'No.'

'Yet, you know who I am.'

'Yes.'

'That doesn't concern you?'

'I don't believe in you, so no.'

The devil scoffed. 'Fucking atheists. Don't expect too much then. If you don't value your soul, I'm not going to give you much for it.'

Casimir thought about the breakfast his growling stomach was after.

'What can I get?'

'What would you like?'

'How 'bout world peace?'

'Fuck off.'

'Yeah, fair enough. I guessed that would be asking too much.'

Casimir wanted to try out his plan, but also wanted to take advantage of the opportunity to ask the Devil some questions.

'Why are you a blur?'

'I take the form people expect of me. Yours must be vague.'

'What's hell like?'

'Fine … for me,' the Devil grinned.

'How often do you get out?'

'Whenever an opportunity like this arises.'

'You mean when someone is seeking you?'

'Yeah.'

'How do you know that's what they're doing?'

'I get a vibe.'

'So you're not omnipresent?'

'No, He above keeps that for himself. I'm wherever I need to be.'

'Sounds efficient.'

'Enough chit-chat. Whaddya want?'

Casimir smothered the grin that was threatening to creep across his face. He believed he could trick the Devil.

'What I want is for all people to develop a lesion in part of their brain, specifically their lateral amygdala, and a thirty percent reduction in their amygdala's volume.'

'That is by far the oddest request I've ever had. What are you playing at?'

'Nothing, I just don't like the amygdala, it's a part of the brain that annoys me and I never know how to pronounce it. I mean is it amy-geh-dala or amig-dala?'

'Are you sure that's all? I mean destroying part of the brain sounds like something I'd do if I had the power to do things that weren't wished for.'

'Ok, I confess—there is more. It's not fair. Women's left ones fire during an argument whereas for men it's the right.'

'So?'

'That helps my wife remember our arguments in lots of detail, whereas I only get the gist. I just want to do something when we argue. If you do what I've asked, it will even the playing field, not just for me, but for all men.'

'You know it will cost you your soul.'

Casimir nodded. The Devil paused as though he was estimating the size of the request.

'I can do that. It would have to be via a virus. Some

people will have a random immunity, but most people will be affected.'

'Give me a percentage. Otherwise, you could make it only a few percent and that won't be enough, uh, um, for men to be free.' Casimir tried not to grimace at his hesitation. He hoped he hadn't given away his deception.

'Fine. Ninety-five percent will be affected.'

'And the rest evenly spread throughout the population.'

'Gee you are specific.'

'I've watched a lot of movies where you've been creative with how the deal was interpreted.'

'Yeah, I do that sometimes.'

'So do we have a deal?'

'One virus that will infect 95% of the population…'

'The world's population.'

'The world's population and the unaffected evenly spread throughout, and…'

'And they'll all be infected within a week and the effect will have occurred one week later.'

'Geez, sure. And in exchange, I get your soul.'

Casimir shrugged, 'Sure. Why not.' He made it sound nonchalant, but inside he was confident he wouldn't lose from this deal.

'We have a deal?'

'Yup.'

They shook hand and what passed for a hand from

the ethereal form.

Casimir smiled. Masked by being a blur, so did the Devil.

#

Two weeks later the virus had done its job. The lesioning and shrinking of people's amygdalae had been completed. At first, no one noticed. In fact, no one noticed for months. Although, Casimir soon realised the Devil had included him in the five percent who weren't affected by the virus. He decided he didn't mind. After all, it was always possible that would be the case. The more he thought about it, the more he imagined that was how the Devil would think he was tricking him. Casimir felt smug. The joke's on you.

The ruse about arguments with his wife was based on a real function of the amygdala. However, the part Casimir had asked to be lesioned wasn't the section which did what he described. Instead, he'd asked for the part that produced the emotion of fear. Casimir knew that without fear, the natural state of people was to be less defensive and more open to others. Now, he could see the change occurring. People were becoming less afraid and were getting on better with each other. People were considerate to others. They were more empathetic. They behaved differently and had what psychologists would call a 'positive affect.' They'd become more enthusiastic, active and alert. In short, Casimir was achieving the goal he had all along—to bring about world peace, despite the Devil telling him he couldn't grant that.

Casimir had been concerned that people might commit more crimes when they weren't afraid, even though the studies he'd read prior to the deal indicated that fearless people were less likely to be convicted of a crime or be the perpetrator of violence. He was pleased that the studies' findings were generalizable to the world's population. Casimir thought back to the flowchart he'd created a few years ago and grinned at the thought he'd found a way to make it a reality.

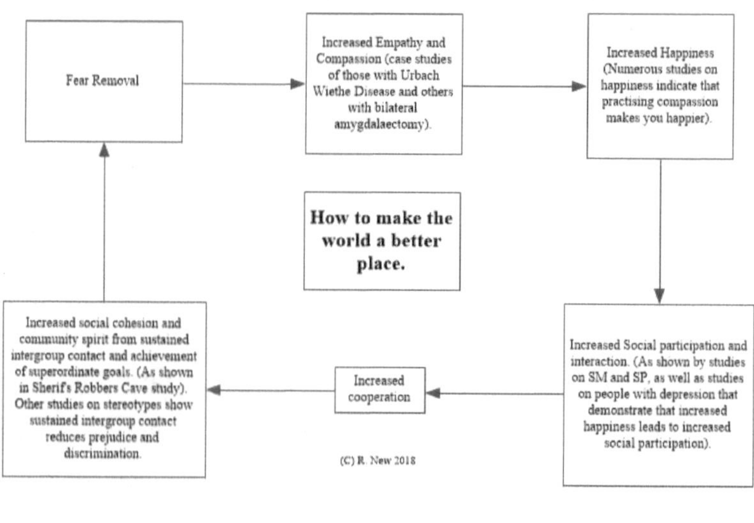


\#

For nearly a year, people were peaceful. Without fear, there was little social tension. This was a different peace than that brought about by the idea of mutually assured destruction, which had prevented countries from attacking each other in the past. This was a real and meaningful cessation of conflict. Casimir was happy, the world was happy, so when the urge to return to One Tree Hill surfaced again, Casimir assumed the Devil was summoning him to try and convince him to reverse their deal. After all, Casimir had managed to disarm evil without resorting to evil.

The trek up the thousand steps felt different to the previous time. Casimir practically floated up, his mood so buoyed by the state of the world. Even the weather felt improved, despite the cloud covering the top of the mountain. The Devil was sitting in the same spot as before. If a blur could grin, the Devil was doing it. Casimir was amused—he must want something.

'So you're back,' said the Devil.

'I assumed you were summoning me.'

'Yeah, I guess I was. I can do that sometimes.'

'What's up? Want to renege on the deal?'

'Not at all. I'm quite happy with the souls you've provided.'

Casimir ignored the plural.

'I wouldn't be too sure you've got mine.'

'Why's that?'

'Matthew 5:9. Blessed are the peacemakers: for they shall be called the children of God. I've brought peace to the world. I don't think…'

'I thought you were an atheist.'

'I guess I was tricking you, but it was for a good cause.'

'Don't be so sure of your righteousness. You've enabled me to do something I've been trying to achieve for millennia—the destruction of the world.'

Casimir laughed. 'The world's the best it's ever been.'

The Devil's silence in response made Casimir suddenly unsure.

'Did you ever wonder why I chose to meet you at this location?'

'No.'

'An open space at the top of a mountain. Where you've had to climb eight hundred and seventy steps…'

'A thousand,' Casimir said indignantly.

'They just call it that. That's why I like making deals with people like you, you think you're smart, but actually you're naïve. This site is where the end of the world begins.'

'I've saved the world,' Casimir said with as much bravado as he could muster. The Devil's confidence worried him.

'No, you've condemned it, and in doing so provided me with more souls than I could've dreamt of.'

'But people are happy and not sinning.'

'True, but that doesn't wipe their slate clean.'

'Why do you think you're about to get their souls?'

'Poor Casimir. You spent so much time thinking

about me being below, you forgot to look up at the sky.'

Casimir dutifully looked upwards. The clouds were moving strangely. They were billowing downwards. Casimir's jaw dropped as he watched the clouds part and an alien spaceship appear. Casimir couldn't move.

'The response you're experiencing used to be called 'fight or flight', because they overlooked 'freeze' as an option. Ironically, it's triggered by your amygdala. In a moment though, you'll be able to run. Now tell me, how do you think people who are unafraid will respond to the aliens?'

'They, they won't do anything,' Casimir stammered.

'That's right. They won't see the aliens as a threat. Even if they start killing, your fearless friends won't see the need to fight back or run away. They're easy pickings.'

An overwhelming horror rose within Casimir as he realised how vulnerable he'd made the planet. A door opened on the spacecraft and some oddly shaped aliens began a controlled descent to the ground.

'They're hostile you know,' the Devil said gleefully.

Casimir finally found his legs. He turned and ran. He had to warn everyone.

The Devil called out after him, 'You won't be able to save them you know.' Casimir only just heard the devil add, 'That's what you get for trying to trick me.'

# Acknowledgements

Despite the view many have of authors, getting ideas into workable stories isn't something that is done by just one person. I am indebted to many people for helping me bring this book to publication. First and foremost is my editor Kathryn Moore, whose guidance and eye for detail were invaluable. Team Juhno did a great job on the cover. Thanks must also go to the members of the Monash Writers Group and my Beta readers: Sophia, Maryann, Robin, Rob, and Sylvia. Their encouragement and feedback on early versions of these stories were immensely useful. I also thank my family since they had to put up with me being grumpy when I couldn't write or got frustrated with a stage of the publishing process. It may be a cliché but I thought about giving up, but then saw who was watching—so thanks to my children Michael and Rachel for keeping me motivated. They get to see Daddy struggle and have setbacks, but ultimately have some wins too.

*The Patriotic Amnesiac* was inspired by the real life study of Henry Molaison (HM) who had his hippocampus removed by a surgeon in an attempt to control his epilepsy. It's interesting to know the surgeon sucked it out with a silver straw. HM was referred to as the perfect amnesiac. I liked this phrase and wondered if I could create a scenario whereby someone would volunteer for such a procedure. The result became *The Patriotic Amnesiac.*

*The Second Fear* and *Devilish Tricks* were based around another psychological study, this one being of SM046. SM046 is a woman who suffers from the fascinating disorder of Urbach-Wiethe disease. She literally cannot feel or recognise fear.

Scientific ideas that interest me, such as liquid metal embrittlement and cloning, inspired some of the other stories. Others were based on a philosophical idea, dream or quirky fact I just had to put into a story.

Some stories have an autobiographical component. John's reaction to Nashida's first miscarriage in *The Doppelganger Gambit* mirrors my own experience when my wife had one—and it really did start on Fathers Day. We are fortunate we'd already had a son, and have since had a daughter. *First Constant* is based on a friend of mine who was killed in the circumstances described in the story. The first half of *La Criminal* is based my experience putting my dog down.

Lastly, the 'intermission' from *The Lost Chapter* largely mirrors my own political views. I intended to write the second act for this latter story, but grudgingly had to admit that it would overlap too much with a novel I have planned, hence Act 2 is presented as it is. Maybe one day I'll get around to writing my version of what it would look like.

Margaret Hepworth has created a lesson plan for teachers based on *How to Win a War*. It's part of her global citizenship education program called The Gandhi Experiment. The teacher resource is available at: http://thegandhiexperiment.teachable.com/p/how-to-win-a-war

If you have enjoyed this book, please rate and review it on Amazon.com, Goodreads, other websites or share your view on social media.

# About the Author

According to his wife, Robert has spent too much of his life studying. She has a point as he's earned seven tertiary qualifications. Robert has degrees in psychology, sociology, biology and education, all of which inspire his writing. He lives in Melbourne with his wife and two children. He likes writing stories that shift the perspective of the reader and that make use of scientific concepts. When he was in high school, a dare escalated a little too quickly and Robert made the state final in an interpretive dance competition.

If you've enjoyed these stories you might also like Robert New's novel *Incite Insight*.

# Incite Insight: Prologue

The Professor was buying breakfast when the reaction started. Intuitively, he knew he didn't have much time. Habit made him start taping his voice.

'I know I am about to die. I cannot control what is happening to me.'

Even as he spoke the first sentence he was aware of the magnitude of what was occurring. If only he could explain what had done this to him so that others might understand. People wandered by, blissfully unaware that the man they were passing was answering the great questions of life. By the time the first thin trickle of blood ran out of his ear, the Professor had already answered 'Who am I?,' proved mankind's existence and outlined a utopian society where everyone was an 'elite' and there were no lower classes. His mind was flooded with information; he could access every memory, every piece of information stored in his brain. Soon he found himself generating new knowledge. As he proved a theory that unified all physical actions, blood began to flow out of his ears, nostrils and eyes. His mouth remained free of blood and he continued to speak. As he spoke words that unlocked the mysteries of life and the universe, the chemicals in his mind reacted so violently his brain was liquefied. For a fleeting second before he died, he'd become a god: able to create, control and exist in all the dimensions of time, awareness and reality.

The people around him would later describe the way he died as looking like his brain had melted.